They danced ~~~~~~~~~~~~~~~~~~~~~~~~~~~~~~~~~~~~ arms
and to feel the ~~~~~~~~~~~~~~~~~~~~~~~~~~~~~~ es on
her cheek, wa~~~~~~~~~~~~~~~~~~~~~~~~~~~~~~ ging
together into ~~~~~~~~~~~~~~~~~~~ to the music from
below and to the startled comment from one of the
soldiers as he looked up and saw them swaying along
the boardwalk, barely visible against the flower-strewn
railings and dim walls.

The fiddle music ended and then began again, this
time with a waltz.

'They don't exist,' Jared murmured as she stopped,
realising that they had been seen. Her cheek returned
to rest against his jacket and they continued to dance.
Nothing mattered. Only Jared and herself . . .

MISTRESS OF TANGLEWOOD

VALENTINA LUELLEN

MILLS & BOON LIMITED
15–16 BROOK'S MEWS
LONDON W1A 1DR

First published in Great Britain 1984
by Mills & Boon Limited

© Valentina Luellen 1984

Australian copyright 1984
Philippine copyright 1984

ISBN 0 263 74998 3

Set in 10 on 11pt Linotron Times
04–0185–62,140

Photoset by Rowland Phototypesetting Ltd
Bury St Edmunds, Suffolk
Made and printed in Great Britain by
Cox and Wyman Ltd, Reading

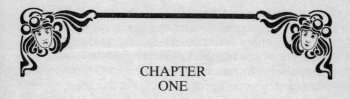

CHAPTER
ONE

'THE YANKEES is coming! Oh, lawd, Miz Holly. The Yankees is here!'

The voice of Mimosa, Holly's maid, as she raced along the magnolia-lined drive towards Tanglewood, could be heard with startling clarity not only inside the thick walls that had housed generations of Beauforts since grandfather Lucien had fled from the threat of the French guillotine to put down new roots in the raw land of South Carolina, but throughout the adjoining gardens, cotton-sheds and slave quarters. As she passed, anxious black faces appeared to follow her progress. Whenever she was agitated, she raised her tones to a pitch somewhere resembling the screech of a sow whose tail had been caught in the pen door and the cockerels that began their raucous chorus at dawn and, for some reason, continued the terrible din for most of the day. Unless one of the yard-boys dampened their male egos with a well-aimed bucket of water.

In a chair drawn up in front of the rosewood writing bureau in the study, where she had fallen asleep over the plantation ledgers for the second time that week, with only three hours' rest to sustain her through another long, arduous day, Holly opened her eyes in alarm. She knew those tones immediately, and inwardly winced at the thought of another false warning.

Yankees, Yankees! They were all the scatterbrained girl thought about. Her mind, full of the ugly stories she had heard from passing soldiers on their way to reinforce Savannah before the city was evacuated, of Sherman's brutal passage through the adjoining state of Georgia, had resulted in her seeing blue-coated uniforms behind every bush and moss-covered tree. Why should they swing north again? What was left for them? They had taken Savannah in December of last year, 1864, after the ten-thousand-strong rebel force there had blown up their ironclads and the navy yard, and disappeared into the waterlogged countryside, leaving the inhabitants at the mercy of the approaching enemy. She had shuddered at that. She had been there only weeks before. Surely now the Union army would press on towards Charleston, into North Carolina, towards—heaven forbid!—the last Confederate stronghold, Richmond.

Not that the city could ever fall to the enemy. But then that confident train of thought faded abruptly as she remembered past events. They should not have taken Atlanta, but they did, with terrible losses to the South. Even reinforced by the Home Guard, young boys and old men who had thought never to pick up a weapon and fight again, the Confederates had again retreated, leaving Georgia open for the Yankees to march through with little or no obstructions. Burning, pillaging, turning people out of their homes, stealing livestock and badly-needed grain. Freeing the slaves who had nowhere to go now, nobody to care for them, and who hung around their so-called liberators in hungry, unkempt, dissatisfied packs. Free and yet not free!

Tanglewood had suffered indirectly from Sherman's rampage. No one had yet seen a blue uniform, and Holly knew that she was not the only one who said a prayer each night that they never would; but their own troops as they retreated, tired, hungry, dispirited, were in dire need of food and warm clothing. The weather had already grown treacherous. Bitterly cold at night, with heavy rainstorms turning the roads into rivers of mud. Already the lower fields, which stretched down to the banks of the Savannah River, had been flooded, uprooting precious new seedlings and young orange-trees. She had spent a whole day there the week before to supervise their removal to higher ground.

At first she had been more than willing to give food and shelter to any soldiers in need, but as the continuous streams began to demand more and more of the chickens meant to see the household through the winter, the hams salted and hung in the smoke-houses, the corn whiskey that old Joseph still insisted on having made, even though there were no men about to drink it any more, she grew almost to resent their appearance. They were hungry now, but if she continued to feed and clothe them, everyone would suffer at Tanglewood in the months to come. The war must end soon, she told herself, but the days still continued to drag by, seemingly with no end to it, and so she began to take store of what provisions they had laid up and ordered even more to be put aside; when the next soldiers arrived she made them welcome and fed them, but sparingly, and made sure all live animals were kept well out of their way.

Until her father returned from the war, she was mistress of the hundred-acre plantation and must make the decisions in his place. It was a burden which had weighed heavily on her shoulders the past year, since the overseer had taken himself off to Atlanta to join up with General Johnston's troops. There were times when she had cried herself to sleep, aching for the strength of her father's arms about her, and the laughter of her two brothers, both dead now, to ease the loneliness which invaded her heart, but those times were past. Tears were of no help. She had taught herself to be strong, to think and act alone. She had forgotten the last time she shed a tear.

'Mimosa, will you hush that noise!' Holly threw open the door, green eyes narrowed against the fierce glare of brilliant sunshine streaming into the hall. Her nerves were taut from lack of sleep, and dark shadows of fatigue showed high in her cheeks. Weeks of playing nurse and waitress to Laurette would sap the energy of the devil himself, she thought somewhat bitterly as she advanced towards the oncoming figure and wished, for the two hundredth time, she had not brought her to Tanglewood. She did not want to be responsible for her brother's widow, whom she did not like and whose airs and graces, within ten minutes of her arrival, had caused an uproar among what little of the household remained. But she was responsible because there was no one else. Clayton was dead and Laurette had no other close relatives to go to; besides, she could not have stayed in Savannah with Sherman's men about to descend on the city. Straightening her shoulders, Holly put all thought of her sister-in-law out of her mind as she caught sixteen-year-old Mimosa by the arm and forcibly detained her.

'Yankees! Down by the river! Miz Holly, we is goin' to be murdered!'

'Be quiet!' Holly shook her, knowing that in her excited state it was impossible to reason with her. 'Listen to me. There are no Yankees. Not here. Not at Tanglewood. We are too far off the main track. You probably saw some of our own men following the river, that's all.'

'No.' Mimosa's eyes rolled like huge saucers. She was clearly terrified, and Holly felt her heart lurch unsteadily. Dear God, it could not be so! Not here, not on her own precious land! 'Down by the river . . . twenty, maybe more. Trampling all over the place with their horses.'

'Did they see you?'

'No, ma'am. I lit out through the swamp grass and cut back here. What we going to do, Miz Holly? There ain't nobody here to protect us. They'll burn the house, steal our food . . .'

'We protect ourselves. Now, no more talk like that. Find Joseph.'

'I'm here, Miz Holly.' A grey-haired negro came out from one of the side rooms which led to the kitchen area. He was one of the oldest men still at Tanglewood. In his sixty-fifth year, he had served the Beauforts man and boy, first as a field hand, then in the house. Now, inside these walls, his word was law. Even Holly rarely disagreed with any decision he made. It helped to take a little of the weight from her shoulders to know here was one person upon whom she could rely implicitly. 'Mimosa's right. They are here. In ten minutes they'll be at the house.'

'Oh, no!' For a moment Holly was seized with panic at visions of the house which had been entrusted to her care being consumed with fire, and the cotton-sheds which stored three years' cotton, stockpiled because they were unable to get it out of Savannah while the Union ships blockaded the port, being set to the torch. Thousands of dollars going up in smoke. All that work for nothing! Animals slaughtered needlessly, looting, and wanton rampaging by the troops. And what would happen to her and Laurette? She had heard stories of how lone women were treated by the enemy, and they had made her chill to the bone.

She must not think of that, or anything else. The

defence of the house first! No, that was impossible. One girl and two pistols against perhaps more than twenty men—trained men. Laurette would be no use. She was still weak after her miscarriage—or said she was. It was over six weeks ago, but she still remained in bed most of the day, insisting on her meals being taken up to her; when she did show herself downstairs, she lazed on the day-bed in the sitting-room until it was time to go up again. No, she would be of no use at all. She was all alone, Holly decided, and wasting precious time.

Joseph's sharp brown eyes considered the stubborn look which descended over her features. Instinctively he knew what she had decided. They had worked as a team for so long that he had begun to find it easy to read her mind.

'I'll fetch the master's pistols from the study. Mimosa, run and find Joshua. Tell him to keep everyone out of the way. Maybe they want only food or a place to stay overnight,' he said in an unruffled tone.

'They will get no welcome here,' Holly said sharply. 'Have you forgotten I have two brothers dead because of them and their damned war?'

Joseph's nose wrinkled slightly to indicate his dislike of her strong language. She was doing the work of a man, and coping well, so over the months he had turned a blind eye to it. If it continued after the return of the Colonel, her father, it would be necessary to remind her, politely but firmly, that no young lady of good breeding ever swore, no matter how upsetting or disturbing the circumstances.

'Bring me my father's pistols, Joseph, and then stay out of sight with the others. This is not your fight, and I don't want you hurt,' Holly instructed, giving Mimosa a push towards the door as she stood hesitating, obviously reluctant to show herself outside again. 'I shall meet them on the porch. What happens after that is up to them. They are not going to destroy my home, I promise you that.'

The man went away, returning with the duelling pistols her father had left behind. Apart from these, there were only two other weapons in the house, and one of those was an ancient musket from the Mexican wars. It hung in Clayton's room and had not been used since he went away. It would not be loaded or primed ready for use. Her eyes widened questioningly as Joseph held out one pistol to her and retained a firm hold on the other.

'If your father was here, I would be proud to stand alongside him, Miz Holly. I was born and raised at Tanglewood. This is my home, too. I'm happy here, and I don't see why anyone should come changing that if I don't want it that way,' he said solemnly.

'My father speaks for me too. I'll stand by you if you'll have me.' The coloured man who stood in the doorway was over six feet and built like a solid oak. Joshua had been acting as her overseer for the past six months. He had proved himself a good worker, as agile with his mind as he was with his hands; the other slaves, those that had not already run away or been taken to dig ditches and fortifications for the Confederates, liked and respected him, despite his promotion. He worked them hard, but no harder than he was willing to work himself, and no longer. Before the war a black overseer would have been unheard-of. Even now, in desperate times, Holly's liberal attitude had brought scathing comments from close friends and neighbours, but so long as the plantation continued to function, she did not care.

She was surprised at the offer. Although they worked in close unison and his father was considered to be more

of a friend than a servant, she suspected that Joshua
had never liked her. At odd times, when she had caught
him watching her, she was sure she had glimpsed something near to contempt in the depths of his dark eyes,
yet he was always civil to her and helpful in his suggestions about the running of the plantation. She could not
fault him, yet still there was something . . .

Without a word, she held out the second pistol. He
took it with a brief nod and established himself by the
door. Outside it had suddenly become very quiet. Even
the cockerels had fallen silent as if they, too, had knowledge of the dreadful event that was about to befall every
single one of the waiting inhabitants.

'Laurette,' Holly gasped. 'I must warn her to stay in
her room.'

Wheeling about, she ran up the stairs two at a time
and rushed without knocking into her sister-in-law's
bedroom.

From the pink and white canopied bed where she
reclined reading an out-of-date magazine, Laurette's
brown eyes rested amusedly on Holly's dishevelled appearance. The blouse and riding skirt were creased
where she had slept in them, her long blonde hair, a
mass of tangled curls, for they had not seen a brush in
over twenty-four hours. Laurette had envied Holly from
the first moment they met.   Envied her position and
money, the men who danced attendance on her without
apparently making one iota of impression. Laurette had
never had any of these things, and she wanted them
with a desperation that had driven her into a loveless
marriage in order to gain them. She wanted to be equal
with Holly Beaufort. Marriage to Clayton had given her
the status she sought, and the money, and a deep
satisfaction in the knowledge that she had deprived the
other girl of the one thing she loved above all else in

the world—even above Tanglewood . . . Clayton, the brother she idolised.

They had been inseparable until she had arrived on the scene and deliberately, with malice aforethought, had forced a wedge between them. Herself! She had taken the place of the sister he had always considered perfect, never missing an opportunity to sing her praises, but she was no replacement and, within one short month of the wedding day, the marriage had already turned sour. Beaufort pride forbade Clayton to confide in anyone, even in his sister, and Laurette, content now that she had everything she wanted, gave not one iota of thought for the man she had used to bring it all about. She had gone her own way, regardless of his feelings.

'Is there a fire somewhere? I heard that stupid girl screaming her head off again. Really, Holly, you should have Joshua take a strap to her.'

'That is not our way,' Holly reminded her sharply. 'She had good reason to be agitated. The Yankees are almost on our doorstep. I suggest you stay here, out of sight. I am going to meet them downstairs and tell them they have no place here.'

'You are going to . . .! Oh, really, Holly, have you taken leave of your senses? You have heard what they are like! Arm the men, what few you can trust. Get them inside the house to protect us,' Laurette insisted, and for a moment her face was tinged with fear. 'Well, don't just stand there! Protect us, for heaven's sake! You must. I'd come down and face them with you, but you know how weak I still am. Oh, if only Clayton were here. He would know what to do.'

Holly inwardly bristled at the use of her dead brother's name. She hurried to the window and looked out over the long drive. Just visible through the dense trees clustered at the far end, she could just make out horses, and men in blue uniforms. Again she had to stem a surge of panic. Stay calm, she told herself. They must never know you are afraid—or alone.

'Don't show yourself,' she said, heading towards the door. 'I have an idea. No man, not even a Yankee, could be callous enough to turn us out of this house when he learns you have just suffered the loss of your baby and are still prostrate with grief over the death of your husband.'

Laurette pulled the patchwork quilt high around her shoulders until only her face showed, her full mouth deepening into an amused smile.

'How do I look?'

'I'm sure that if they come up here you can convince them of your frailty,' Holly retorted, and was instantly ashamed at the antagonism pushing its way to the surface.

'You should have been a man. You think like one. Did Clayton ever suspect what a devious mind his sweet little angelic sister has?' Laurette asked, eyes glinting maliciously. Holly left her without an answer, and rejoined the two men waiting downstairs.

'They are here,' Joshua said, as she reached the bottom of the stairs.

Her fingers reached into the pocket of her skirt and touched the tiny Derringer Clayton had given her for her eighteenth birthday. He had taught her to use it, without her father's knowledge, for he would never have considered it seemly for her to be seen handling a pistol. She had hidden it away in a closet in her bedroom, never dreaming that one day she would have need of it. But the day had come, and she was prepared to use it to defend her home, and her life, if necessary.

'Open the doors, Joseph. We do not want them broken down.' She heard the sound of many horses on the drive, the jangle of harnesses, and a harsh voice barking orders. Straightening her shoulders, she stepped forward into the sunlight, Joseph on one side of her, Joshua on the other. Head held high, face taut with emotion, she steeled herself to remain composed as the first Union soldiers dismounted before Tanglewood. Framed in the huge brass-studded doorway, flanked by two impassive black faces, she waited. And that was how Jared Ruell first saw her! Proud! Defiant and twenty years old!

Major Jared Ruell was tired, disillusioned and still damp from the heavy rain-storm the previous night. This had necessitated him having to sleep in wet clothes that clung to his body all night long, as his regiment camped along the banks of the Savannah, before moving on to join the forces of General Sherman, en route to Columbia.

Tired, disillusioned and angry at his encroachment upon yet another seemingly undefended plantation that he would be forced, under orders, to destroy! Dear God, would this war never end? After three years of continual fighting, and the needless destruction of lives and property that only brought him endless nightmares night after night, he would have been glad—relieved—to make the journey to Columbia unopposed.

Unopposed! He stared at the huge white house ahead of him, magnificent in its structure. Its defiance! All was silent as he and his men rode the mile-long avenue to it. Tall trees bending above his head, leaves entwined, made a sun-dappled arched bough. Of welcome? No. Here, neither he nor his men were welcome, for they wore the wrong uniforms. What would he find here? Out-of-date muskets? Wounded Confederates, more concerned with the planting of spring corn than their own welfare? Old men, women, haggard before their time? Youngsters full of hatred? Black faces welcoming their arrival, demanding unobtainable dreams?

How tired he was! How unable to cope with his own sparse needs, let alone those of his men and the hangers-on. He had at least fifty negroes, a third of them women and children, many babes in arms, acquired during the long, deplorable trek through Georgia. They looked to him for so many things he could not give them. Freedom was not enough. They wanted reassurance, hope for the future. How could he give them that, when he had none for himself?

His brother David had been right to stay out of the war, but then he had not had the strong hand of their father behind him, prompting, or rather pushing, him into a way of life totally alien to him. Jared had proved himself during the long years spent in wild untamed Indian territory after leaving West Point Military Academy, had hated the army then enough to leave it, vowing never to return. But he had. When it was demanded of him, by a father who idolised him and whom he revered above all men. For him, the dignity of his name and his past deeds, Jared had become a callous destroyer of life and property! For *him*, he had forgotten what it was like to be a human being. Duty came first! War destroyed people! War destroyed integrity—and honour—and love! War brought to the forefront of human nature its basic instincts. How to kill and how to survive!

One day it would end, but Jared knew he would never be the same again. Sometimes, when he lay awake at night, cold with sweat evoked by his memories, he wondered if there was a single spark of humanity left in him. Serving under General William Tecumseh Sherman, now in command in the west, he doubted it. That man revelled in what he did. When the Union army had marched triumphantly into Savannah last December, Jared had been sick at heart. For him there was no celebrating. He had seen too much death and destruction, too many dead bodies lying in the sun, far too many widows watching as his men herded them from their homes and threw in the lighted torches. Deprived of even a roof over their heads, often food for their mouths. Old men, women and children starving because of Sherman's policies. This was not war. It was revenge on a people he neither liked nor understood. Jared held no views on slavery. He had seen both sides of the coin since the war began. Good and bad . . . the North was no different in his eyes.

The report put out by General Sherman deepened his disgust at what was happening all through the South. The damage done to Georgia and its military resources was estimated at millions of dollars. How it haunted him, all that waste and destruction. The burning of beautiful old houses, badly needed cotton which would have seen the South back on its feet again when the war was over, the inhuman treatment of the old and sick. Women young and old. He wanted no more of it. A thousand times he had prayed for the war to end. It must soon. The South was beaten. How their men still fought on, ragged, starving, without reinforcements was a mystery to him. He still fought them when and where he found them, for above all—albeit against his will—he was a soldier, but he had grown to respect the enemy and their magnificent will to survive.

At the beginning of February 1865, Sherman was on the move again, this time heading towards Columbia in South Carolina. The order went out to treat this State, which had led the secession movement, as harshly as Georgia. Jared Ruell rode out of that city bitter of mind and heavy of heart. He would obey those orders, but as God was his witness, he would never forgive himself for the sorrow and misery he caused along the way. Nor did he want forgiveness. This terrible burden would lie on his shoulders for the rest of his life, unless in some way he could redeem himself and all he had done in the past. It was a vain hope—for a soldier!

Jared signalled his men to halt, and drew rein himself before the imposing mansion. It was as quiet as a grave-yard. No sign of life, apart from the three motionless figures on the white-painted porch. Two armed negroes and a slip of a girl. It was the first time he could remember having encountered coloureds with weapons. At least, weapons with which they were prepared to defend their masters and their families. All too often they turned on them, using hatchets, scythes, pick-axes, anything destructive enough to show their hatred of the people who had held them in subservience for so long. These men were different, he suspected, viewing them through narrowed gaze. They meant business! They were prepared to defend the girl between them against any odds, and it had to be their own decision. With weapons in their hands, she stood no chance at all if they changed their minds. No orders on God's earth could have saved her life. So frail-looking, yet she commanded the respect of an old man and a giant of a negro who could have split her in two with his bare hands had he wished to do so. She shared something with them that Jared had not encountered before, and it made him curious.

Defiance was written on all three faces. God! These Southerners and their damned pride! Elsewhere in the South, what he had seen of it at least, the coloured slaves had been only too willing to rise, to leave their wretched hovels and join behind the army that they believed had come solely to free them. In the one or two opposite cases he had seen, he had been struck, as he was now, by the intense loyalty between servant and master. Somewhere between the two there must have been the solution for peace between the North and the South. Could no one else see it? He had eventually accepted that they could not. Indians or negroes—to politicians, they were all the same. Besides, no politicians ever ventured into a war zone. They valued their necks too highly to risk them by going to see the havoc government policies were having on the people and country.

'Lieutenant Rhys. Take six men and look around,' he ordered the officer at his side. 'If there is no resistance offered, I want no trouble. Is that clearly understood?'

'Yes, sir.' The man wheeled his horse away, snapping out orders and names in sharp, clipped tones. Jared watched him ride round the back of the house, deliberately guiding his mount over grass and flowers alike. Young, ambitious and enjoying every moment of this campaign among people he despised. Under the right command, he would go far. Jared disliked him intensely, but he was a good second-in-command, if you watched your back.

Luckily he had someone to do that for him. This was the big-framed Irishman, built like a barrel and able to consume as much liquor as one contained, who rode always at his left hand, and had done since they had met after Jared's graduation from West Point and subsequent posting to the wilds of New Mexico at his own request. Raw, inexperienced, desperately needing guidance, he had not been too proud to accept it, as many of his associates had been.

He had gained a wealth of knowledge from the craggy-faced Patrick Wayne, Irish to the core and willing to fight anyone who cast a slur on his beloved homeland, even though he had never seen Ireland, having been born and raised in New Jersey, of immigrant parents. He was contemptuous of rank. Hard-drinking, hard-swearing, and insubordinate to those above him who had seen less service or to whom he took a dislike for one reason or another—which was why he was still a sergeant, losing his stripes and regaining them more times than Jared could recall. Over-loyal to the extent of putting his own neck, which he considered of prime importance, on the line for anyone he liked. Jared never knew why they had become such close friends. Wayne, more than Tim Rhys, was his right hand, steadfast and trusted to the death. And, from a soldier, no more could be asked than that he give up his life for you!

Wayne had been in the army for thirty-two years. He had seen gold-braided officers come and go, and survived their often egotistical commands, obeyed their inane orders and somehow extricated himself from the most difficult situations. He knew people. He watched, listened and assessed without a word. Out of sight of the brass hierarchy, he was feared throughout the ranks. His word was law, and, thanks to his greater experience, many men had come through the last four years who might otherwise not have survived—Jared among them.

Once, among the Navaho, when they were on the trail of Manolito in 1860, the sergeant had saved his life under particularly gruesome circumstances. Again, as they came up against the dogged troops of General Johnston retreating towards Atlanta, and Jared's horse had been downed by cannon-fire that pinned him stunned and bleeding beneath it, Patrick Wayne had been at his side, to cover him with protective fire as he stumbled reeling to his feet and caught another riderless horse to make good his escape. He had wondered many times, since that day, what would happen on the third occasion? His time was running out.

Jared, too, had learned to watch people over the years. In this way he had quickly realised that Tim Rhys was to be neither trusted nor relied upon. Too ambitious for his own good, he was oblivious to the needs of the men fighting alongside him. Selfish and arrogant. The potential which could have made him a leader had been destroyed by these two things. There were times when Jared Ruell felt very much alone.

Never more than he did now, as he faced the three figures on the porch. Slowly he dismounted, ignoring Wayne's warning frown, and mounted the steps towards them. His men were as tired as he was. They could do with a few days' rest and good food before continuing their journey. He shut out the nagging uneasiness at the back of his mind that suggested he was merely putting off the inevitable unpleasantness which would follow his departure. What if he was? A few more days, either way, would not affect the war. For the South it had been over long ago.

It was not over for this girl, or her companions, he thought, looking into their closed faces. Damn them, were they going to make it difficult for him?

'What do you want here?' Holly demanded. How calm she sounded. In control of herself and the situation. Nothing could have been further from the truth.

'To begin with, it might ease the hostility in the air a little if you told your men to put down their weapons,' Jared said, halting only a few paces from her, but being careful not to put himself directly in the line of fire. He knew that Wayne had drawn his sidearm the moment his feet touched the ground.

She could not have been more than nineteen or twenty. Little fool! It was obvious that there were no men about or they would have shown themselves by now. A deserted plantation, a couple of trusted negroes and a young girl, foolishly trying to act like a man in a situation far beyond her limited control. Damned if she did not have more courage than most men he had met, he thought with begrudging admiration.

Stop hedging, Jared! Get on with it before you start feeling sorrier for this one than all the rest. There is nothing you can do!

Behind the three figures, the open doors showed polished wood floors and gleaming furniture. Like shadows, Lieutenant Rhys and two men had stolen in through a back entrance and taken up positions a few feet away, pistols aimed at the unsuspecting backs. One word from him! One false move from the men or the girl!

She had said nothing in answer to his demand. His lips tightened.

'My name is Ruell, ma'am. Major Jared Ruell. I want—and this is not a polite request.' Best to let her know how things were from the start. 'I want quarters for myself, my lieutenant and sergeant, and a suitable place for my men to bed down. We shall be resting here for a few days. You will supply us with whatever food and other necessities we require. And before you think of risking the lives of your two servants, you should know that there are three pistols behind you. Isn't that right, Rhys?'

'Quite right, Major.'

He saw Holly wince at the voice from behind which signalled an end to her brave, but futile, stand. Jared's eyes met and locked with hers. Slate grey, as cold as naked steel, challenging blazing green fire. Challenged —and won, as her gaze faltered and fell. For a minute before he realised the advantage was his, he felt as though he were teetering on the edge of a chasm. One foolish step, and he would surely fall, bringing about his own destruction.

During the last four years of war he had been through various relationships, most of them exceedingly short-lived, with women whose names he had either not known or had forgotten the moment he left their beds. Never had he experienced such an overwhelming, inexplicable, surge of desire. It leapt unbidden between them like a naked flame, and he knew by the tell-tale flush of colour which stole into the girl's pale cheeks that it was not his imagination. She had felt it, too!

A spot of rain on his cheek reminded him of the discomfort of his clothes and of the men behind him who were also anxious to find dry shelter before the heavens opened again, which, by the look of the black clouds above them would be any minute.

'I'm out of time and patience,' Jared snapped.

'Joseph, put down your pistol. You too, Joshua,' Holly said quickly, aware this was no bluff. The man facing her, she suspected, was a hardened soldier who had seen and killed many people. Two more corpses, perhaps three, would not perturb him. They obeyed reluctantly, Joshua's face a mask of indecision, which surprised her. He was free now to go with these soldiers if he wished, to take Mimosa with him as his woman. With sudden startling clarity she realised that he did not want to leave the plantation. Like his father, he had a measure of power, a position to uphold here. As a freed slave he would have neither, nor a home, nor clothes for his back, nor work. Sergeant Wayne stepped forward and relieved the two men of their weapons. He sensed that Jared was relieved by the capitulation, although no one else was aware of it. 'You cannot stay in this house, Major Ruell.' Holly was adamant. The suggestion was out of the question. 'As you have so correctly guessed, there are no men here other than my servants and field hands. And my sister-in-law is sick upstairs . . .'

'Sergeant, see the men are bedded down in those sheds we passed. They are to conduct themselves in an orderly manner at all times, if possible without trampling over everything in sight,' Jared ordered. 'And if I hear of any woman being molested against her will, I'll hang the man responsible from the nearest tree.'

Not for one moment did Holly believe he would carry out such a threat. He was trying to put her off guard. A young man in lieutenant's uniform moved into view, holstering his sidearm, and she coloured hotly at the boldness of his gaze.

'No sign of resistance, Major. And, from what I can see, plenty of food for us all and grain for the horses. There's a stream running at the back of the house behind the slave cabins. Most of them are half empty,' Tim Rhys said, still contemplating Holly's red cheeks. He wondered what the other one upstairs was like.

'That food and grain is all we have,' Holly protested. 'You can't take any of it. We have to live through the winter . . .'

'You said your sister-in-law was sick. I have a doctor following behind with the supply wagons.' Jared ignored her outburst. 'Where is she?'

'In her room, of course.' What a cold-hearted monster he was, she thought. She judged his age to be somewhere in the early thirties. There were no streaks of grey yet in the thick black hair just visible beneath his hat. Perhaps a few years younger, but the weathered features made it difficult to be more accurate.

The mouth was firm. The jaw square cut and betraying a hint of ruthlessness, as though he was a man accustomed to having his own way. A man who gave orders and expected them to be obeyed without question, she supposed. The slate-grey eyes surveying her were without pity for her predicament, and suddenly she realised she was very much afraid of Jared Ruell.

'Show me.' It was an order, not a request.

Joseph stiffened as the officer stepped towards the open door. With a faint shake of her head, Holly indicated that he was to do nothing. Squaring her shoulders, she turned and went into the house.

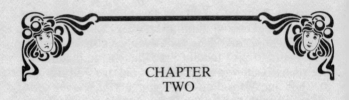

CHAPTER
TWO

Up THEY went, past ancient ancestors who hung in their
gilt frames, staring blank-eyed at the blue-coated figure
following Holly up the wide, sweeping staircase. If they
could speak now, she was sure they would damn her
soul to the eternal fires of hell for not having him shot
when she had the chance, but that would have meant
the lives of two innocent men who sought only to protect
her. Had she died, too, that would have left Tanglewood
at the mercy of enemy troops, to be ransacked, burned,
desecrated. Her fingers curled tightly round the stock
of the Derringer in her pocket as Jared asked from
behind her,

'Are your men at the war?'

She paused on the landing to look at him, anger and
bitterness in her reply. Sadness in her lovely face.

'My two brothers are dead. My father is—somewhere.
I don't know where. Since your General Sherman took
Savannah, we have heard nothing of the war. I was
beginning to hope that he had had enough of death and
destruction, and we would be left alone.'

'You shall be, if you give me no trouble,' Jared said,
and instantly cursed himself for making stupid promises
he could not keep. If it was up to him, he would rest
his men and then move them on, but it was not. He had
his orders. Like it or not, he was a soldier until the war
was over.

'You have a smooth tongue, Major, but don't waste

your time with lies. You are no different from those
soldiers who marched through Georgia, burning, pillaging, raping. Perhaps you were one of them.'

'My men and I came through that State.' He did not
bother to lie, and saw her flinch as if he had struck her.
Without a word, she continued on her way along a
corridor where more pictures hung on the walls. Not of
disapproving kin, but landscapes of the country around
Tanglewood and many of the house itself.

'These are fine paintings,' Jared observed, admiring
the white house set against a bleak winter background,
and alongside it, in contrast, dainty pink and white
magnolia blossoms and wistaria shading parts of the
white stone from view. Another showed the house from
a different angle in autumn: the muted hues of brown
and yellows had been skilfully blended to produce a
picture projecting warmth of great intensity.

'My brother Clayton painted them. He loved this
place. He had such plans for it . . . He was killed in the
defence of Atlanta,' Holly ended abruptly, opening the
door to Laurette's room. He had not denied he had
been in Georgia. He might even have fired the bullet
responsible for the death of the brother she adored. She
hated his uniform, and she hated him. He was a cold,
ruthless soldier who cared nothing for her needs or
those of Laurette or the negroes who relied on her to
feed and clothe them. 'Laurette, don't be afraid. It's
only me. I have a Union officer with me, and he insists
on seeing you.'

Not that her sister-in-law would be afraid, Holly
thought, as she entered the room and moved towards
the bed. The eyes which regarded the man at her side
were curious more than anything else. The clothes were
tucked high around her shoulders in a most demure
manner. For a moment she did not speak, then,

'Yankees! Here! Oh, Holly, what is to become of us?' she asked in a hushed voice. Her eyes, now wide and apprehensive, had a tear in each one. Holly gave her full marks for acting, even though she felt like slapping her.

'My sister-in-law, Laurette Beaufort. Clayton's widow.' Jared remained silent, and she realised she had not told him her own name. She did so with great reluctance. 'I am Holly Beaufort.'

'As prickly as your namesake,' Jared replied humourlessly. Stepping past her, he bent over the bed and laid a hand against Laurette's cheeks.

'What ails her? I don't want my doctor wasting his time. We have wounded men with us.' He straightened again with a heavy frown.

'Then do not trouble him,' Holly flashed, stung by his callousness. 'Laurette miscarried in December. The shock of Clayton's death. She was ill for several weeks, then this bad weather brought on a chest cold. We ran out of medicines months ago and it is impossible to get any more. With our railway-lines blown up it is impossible to get *anything* these days,' she added meaningfully, and Jared threw her a narrowed look. If his judgment was correct, there was nothing wrong with the other girl. Not now, at least. If anyone needed medical attention, it was Holly Beaufort herself, he thought, as she turned away and coughed for several minutes into a handkerchief. Her face looked gaunt and full of stress, and for the first time he noticed the dark lines of tiredness beneath her eyes. He had seen that look before on the faces of captured rebels. Men driven to the limit of their endurance, exhausted, yet somehow still defiant, gathering strength from some tiny spark to fight on.

'She'll have medicine if it is necessary. Now, my

requirements. Rooms for myself and two others. What else is on this floor?' he asked, following her back into the corridor.

'My own two rooms, my brothers' and my father's. Upstairs are the servants' quarters.'

'Show me.' Again it was an order, not a request.

Balefully Holly glared at him, but obeyed. He selected Clayton's room for Rhys, his lieutenant, despite her protests. Robert's room for the sergeant. She closed her mind to the thought of them being used by the enemy. When they had gone, she would burn the bed-linen and clean them from top to bottom.

'What is this?' Jared opened another door and looked into a spacious, pleasant room with large windows that overlooked the lawns and paddocks. His men were milling below, unsaddling horses, unloading wagons, putting up their bivouacs—being helped, he saw, by several negroes. So they were coming out of hiding.

'You can't have this one. It's . . . it's not used now. Besides, it adjoins my own rooms,' Holly declared indignantly, and he looked across at her, his lip curling amusedly. 'It would not be right—or proper. My father's room is . . .'

'This one will be fine. You have nothing to fear, Miss Beaufort. I'm too damned tired to think about what's on your mind, but, if you are concerned, I am willing to lend you a pistol at night.'

'That won't be necessary, Major. I am quite capable of taking care of myself and I am an excellent shot,' Holly returned, a sharp edge to her tone, and Jared found himself looking down the ugly barrels of a twin Derringer.

She held it confidently; her hand steady, he saw, and he knew she could use it. He reproved himself for not

having searched her when they came upstairs. Did she
intend to shoot? Her expression told him nothing.
Another brave gesture of defiance, or of intention?

'Give me that toy before someone gets hurt,' he
ordered, stepping towards her.

'Don't!' Holly warned. She had not intended to shoot
him, only to show him that she would not be treated
like other women he had encountered. Now, as she held
the Derringer, she realised—one slight squeeze of the
trigger and he would be dead! It would be so simple.
Clayton and Robert avenged with one stroke.

In that split second, as she hesitated, Jared's arm
swept upward and lean brown fingers with the strength
of steel in them coupled her wrist, thrusting it aside.
The Derringer was snatched from her grasp. Through
vision blurred with tears, she saw his face and was
suddenly afraid. It was like a mask carved out of granite,
and set in it were the slate-grey slits that served for eyes.
She turned to run, but he was too quick and his frame
blocked the doorway.

'So you'd like to kill me, would you? You are not the
first. If you get another chance before I leave, you'd
better be sure you are prepared to use your weapon
before you point it at me. The next time I won't be so
gentle.'

Gentle! She tentatively applied shaking fingers to her
bruised wrist. As quickly as the anger had come, it
drained from him at the sight of the marks his fingers
had left on her soft skin. Now he had given her reason
to hate him.

In silence he unloaded the Derringer, paused, and
then slipped a single bullet back into one chamber
before holding it out to Holly. Confused, bewildered,
she made no move to take it. What game was he playing
now?

'One is all you will need to kill me, but remember what I said before you attempt it.'

He expected her to refuse, she thought. She took the weapon without a word and returned it to her pocket, although she knew she would never have the courage to threaten him with it again. Well done, Jared thought. Bruised, but not beaten. He sincerely hoped she would not try it again.

He turned away and returned to the window. He was going to enjoy this beautiful view for the next few days, whether she liked it or not. Four days, five at the most. He had wounded men who needed to rest. It was excuse enough to linger longer than necessary.

'How many slaves have you?' he demanded without looking round.

Holly stared at his broad back, slowly gathering her composure. Neither her father nor brother had ever laid hands on her, except in play. Her wrist would be bruised, she thought. Animal! She was beginning to understand how those poor Georgians had felt the moment they saw a blue uniform.

'About a hundred. There were more, but some have run off. Others . . .' she shrugged slim shoulders. Why should she explain to him? It was none of his business.

'Do you have an overseer? A place as large as this usually does.'

'He left to enlist when Atlanta was beseiged. I've managed alone since then. I have one of the darkies in his place for the moment. Not all of them want to run off, you know,' she ended sarcastically, and Jared turned and stared at her, his lips pursed.

'I know that, Miss Beaufort. The fact that I wear blue instead of grey doesn't make me a fool. Why don't you just accept that we are here to stay for a few days? You behave yourself, and we shall, too.'

'And when you leave?' He saw her lips trembled as she asked the question. She was no fool either. She suspected the worst and knew he would not confirm it. Nor did he.

'Then you can continue your life as usual,' he returned without hesitation.

'Major, sir.' Wayne stood in the doorway, a middle-aged man in a stained white coat behind him, puffing on an evil-smelling old pipe. Holly's nose wrinkled in disgust and she moved slightly to one side. 'I took the liberty of bringing the doctor for the sick woman.'

'Second door on your left along the hall,' Jared said. 'Perhaps you would like to show him, Miss Beaufort, and then you can go about your business. I'm sure you have things to do. If you leave the house area, however, I insist on an escort. Is that clearly understood?'

'I am a prisoner?' Holly asked, aghast.

'It is merely a precaution. There are deserters from both sides wandering the countryside. A lone woman is vulnerable, you must accept that. I have no intention of interfering with your daily routine, believe me.'

'I would as soon believe the devil himself,' Holly retorted with a toss of her head which sent the cloud of loose hair tumbling about her shoulders like a torrent of gold.

Wayne stepped aside to allow her to pass, and then looked at Jared, his weathered face creased into a broad smile.

'That one has a temper. What's the other one like?'

'A lazy slut is my first opinion. I could be wrong, but I doubt it. She'd sell her soul to stay warm and comfortable. Just the type Rhys likes.'

'And the blonde one?'

'We shall have trouble with her when we leave. What kind of place is it?'

'Well cared for. The negroes are, too. The cabins look clean, and families have been kept together. About half of them have come over to us already, the others look as if they prefer to stay where they are. It's their home, they say, where else would they go?'

'Where else, indeed,' Jared sighed, turning back into the room. He would appreciate the view late this afternoon. Now he had things to do. 'Are the men settling in?'

'They are fine. Some bedded in the barns, others outside. The cooks are preparing a meal. The best we've eaten for a long while, Major.'

'Good. Your room is across from mine. Don't get too comfortable in it; I want you on duty tonight in case of trouble. I don't anticipate any, but I'm not sure of the lie of the land yet. Tomorrow I want you and Lieutenant Rhys out on a patrol. I want to know how many, if any, plantations there are in this area. You know what you have to do if you come across resistance.'

'I do that, Major. Does she know?' Wayne asked, meaning Holly. 'Did you tell her this place would be going up in flames when we leave?'

'No. I don't know about you, Wayne, but I've had a basinful of Sherman's torch policy. I'll think about what has to be done when we leave, and not one second sooner,' Jared said, searching through his pocket for a cigar, and then remembering that he had smoked the last one when he was wet through the night before. 'See if you can find me some smokes, will you? And water for a bath about noon. I'm going out to ride around, as soon as I've changed.'

'I'll come with you, sir.'

'No, I want you here to keep an eye on Rhys and the men. A few hours' peace and quiet, Sergeant, that's all I ask. Can you manage that?'

'You'll have it, Major. That's a promise.' He knew

Jared was going to ride in the wooded countryside they had come through after leaving the banks of the Savannah. Alone with his thoughts, his memories. It was a small thing to ask.

'That horrible, smelly little man,' Laurette declared for the tenth time since Holly had entered the room. 'It was humiliating! Lord's sakes, Holly, help me with these hooks, I'm stuck.'

Holly obliged in silence, wondering what the doctor had said to bring about such a miraculous recovery in such a short time. Within an hour after he had left her, Laurette had been out of bed. She fastened the hooks of the dress, her thoughts elsewhere after a moment. Joshua had given her bad news. At least half of the hands were refusing to go about their normal duties. They had begun to hang about the soldiers. Some of the younger, prettier women had caught the eyes of some of them and refused to budge from their sides. His one and only attempt to remind them who and what they were was shouted down by raucous criticism. They were free now, able to think for themselves, go where they pleased, with whom they pleased!

Free, Holly thought, wondering how she would get through the spring ploughing so short-handed. Everyone would just have to work twice as hard. That included herself and Laurette. Now she was on her feet again, she would be put to good use. Those that wanted to go with the soldiers could do so—she would be well rid of them. She would manage, somehow. Thank heavens for Joseph and Joshua. She knew she could count on those two, no matter what happened. That left cook and the three kitchen-maids. She was not at all sure of those, and discounted them. Mimosa would stay with Joshua if she had the choice. Three, perhaps four, trusted servants and forty or fifty field hands who relied on her more than she did on them. If only she had a strong shoulder to lean on, someone to tell her troubles to, just once!

'Holly, are you daydreaming? Don't tell me that handsome Major has turned your head already?' Laurette declared, spinning around in front of the mirror, scrutinising her slim waist. At last she was back to normal size again. She had not liked being pregnant, even though the child she carried belonged to the man she had loved.

'I have more important things to think about than Major Ruell, and you have, too. As you are feeling better, you can help downstairs while I am out in the fields. We are left with fewer than half the darkies, so I shall be away from the house longer than usual. You will have to supervise the kitchen and tell cook about meals. I shall be far too busy to deal with it.'

'What about him?' Laurette almost argued at the thought of such menial tasks being allotted to her, then, considering the advantages for a moment, she remained silent on the subject, a smile touching her sensuous mouth. 'Where will the Major be having his meals? And the others he installs here? With us?'

'Certainly not!' Holly retorted indignantly. 'I cannot bring myself to be civil to him, let alone eat in his detestable presence.'

'Then you are a fool,' Laurette said, her smile fading. 'You will bring trouble for all of us. We are two women alone, do you need reminding of that—and they are men—lonely men away from their homes and their wives and families. For the short time they are here, we must be accommodating. Civil, pleasant in our manner, no matter what we feel about them. Make them welcome, Holly, or they will raze this place to the ground before they go and treat us like common whores.'

'You are suggesting I should act like one, anyway. I can't. I loathe the sight of them.' Holly was openly shocked by the suggestion.

'Poor Holly, you have so much to learn about men. They are like children if you know how to handle them,' Laurette said with a soft laugh.

'You would know more about that than I.' Holly turned away towards the door, bristling at the idea of her being 'nice' to Jared Ruell. 'If you don't need me any more, I have work to do. Are you coming down now?'

'But of course. As you say, I must accept my share of the load until things improve. Really, Holly, it is nothing like as disastrous as you make out. I shall quite enjoy entertaining our guests.'

'I did not ask you to do that,' Holly snapped, tight-lipped. 'Have you forgotten you are recently widowed? Did my brother mean so little to you?'

'He meant a great deal, my dear—at the time. But he is dead now and my grief cannot last for ever, and here at Tanglewood there are no disapproving matrons tutting at my every move.' She spun round in front of the mirror again, patting her brown curls into place. She wore a dress of dark red velvet which set off the chestnut hues in her hair. 'I shall not wear black, nor shall I pretend something for Clayton that I never felt. You always were a good judge of character, Holly. You knew from the start what I was really after—and I got it, didn't I?'

Holly fled from the room, from the malicious smile on Laurette's face, from the terrible urge to hit her for desecrating the memory of her dead brother with such callous words. Her only hope was that he had died without knowing the truth.

She swallowed the indignant remark which rose to her lips, as she ordered her horse to be saddled for her to ride out into the fields and see if the rain had done more damage to the new seedlings. Having mounted, she found herself flanked on either side by two blue-uniformed figures. Joshua, seeing her outraged face, swung himself back into the saddle and said he would ride with her. As protection, she wondered, or to show his authority—black authority here? For whichever reason, she was grateful for his company. She did not like the way her guards looked her over.

It did not take long for her to forget the odious presence of the soldiers. The flooded river was receding, but it would be several weeks, if the weather did not improve, before the spring ploughing could begin. She glanced doubtfully at the overcast sky. It looked as grey and heavy as her heart felt, but she had to bear it. She voiced loud, but ignored, protests when the last of the oranges were stripped from the trees and taken back to the other soldiers. How much more would be stolen from under her nose before they left, she wondered. There was anger on Joshua's face too, she noticed. He caught her puzzled look, and immediately his expression became unreadable. He did care! If only she could reach him a little more. At this moment they shared so much! Tanglewood was the home of them both. She sensed that he would back her in whatever she did in order to protect it, yet he said not one word in support. As proud as she was, she realised, and as stubborn. One day . . .

Tired out, she mounted the steps to the house to find it ablaze with lights. The last of their precious candles, she thought, horrified, and stalked into the sitting-room, recriminations rising to her lips. They died there at what she saw. Lieutenant Tim Rhys lounged in her father's chair in front of the huge fireplace where, for the first time in weeks, a fire blazed cheerfully, welcoming her as it had done at the end of the day when they would all retire after dinner to sit and talk. And he was drinking her father's brandy! This was too much. Across the room, Jared watched the anger which crossed her face. It intensified as her gaze reached him and she realised he had found her father's Havana cigars.

'Holly, I was hoping you would be back in time to dine with us.' Laurette rose from a chair at the side of the lieutenant and came towards her, smiling cordially.

Holly stared daggers at the two uniformed figures before her, overwhelmed by a bitterness and humiliation such as she had never known before. If only she had been born a man! The sight of Laurette, beautifully gowned, smelling of Parisian perfume which she had bought when Clayton took her there for their honeymoon, taunted her beyond reason. She had gone over to their side, the side of the enemy, in order to survive. A traitor!

She flung the word at the other girl and saw her flinch slightly, but her composure returned immediately. The smile came back to her face, the derision to her eyes, as she considered Holly, pale-cheeked, worn out from her ride, her clothes damp from the shower which had caught them an hour before.

'My poor dear, go and have a hot bath and then put on something pretty and come down to eat with us. I cannot handle two impetuous gentlemen alone.'

'No, thank you, Laurette, I shall have Mimosa bring me a tray in my room. I shall not be missed. As for coping with these two "gentlemen" . . .' She laid heavy emphasis on the last word, and saw Jared's eyebrows rise mockingly. Let him laugh at her, damn him! She would not lower herself to Laurette's level. 'They are no more gentlemen than you are a lady.'

And with that she turned on her heel and left Laurette standing open-mouthed and, probably for the first time in her life, at a loss for words. As she started upstairs she heard deep-throated laughter behind her and knew, without looking back, that it came from Jared Ruell. He would laugh on the other side of his face before he left Tanglewood, she vowed. Not tonight, she was too tired, but tomorrow, or the day after, she would show him! Not Laurette's way, she was not capable of that. Or was she?

In her room, after she had washed the grime from her face and hands and slipped into a warm fur-trimmed robe, she sat before the table with her supper tray, and pondered the thought. She was as pretty as Laurette—more so, if she believed all she had been told by the local beaux who had courted her. She had never been interested in getting married, or having children. She wanted to run Tanglewood, to share it with her father and brothers. That was all that had ever mattered to her. Now, for this moment anyway, it was all hers, and she was suddenly beginning to realise what she had been deprived of. The boys who had courted her, flirted with her, had gone off to war. She would not see many of those faces again. If any. Most of them had gone into Georgia and would never return to their homes, to the mothers and sisters who waited hopefully, but in vain, for a sight of their dear faces. She had lost two brothers. Perhaps a father. So far no bad news, but she had heard nothing of the war for so long. Major Ruell could provide all the facts she did not want to know, but accepted that she must. But in order to discover them, she would have to be polite to him. Laughter drifted up to her from downstairs. She picked at her food and pushed it away. Laurette and Yankees! Clayton was better off dead than knowing what she was. No, that was not the truth. Alive, he would be at Tanglewood with his sister. Laurette was of secondary importance only.

She could not sleep. She had climbed into bed just after nine, but tossed and turned for more than two hours. More laughter from below. It was deliberate, she suspected. Laurette was having her revenge for the remarks she had endured, knowing full well that Holly's room was above the sitting-room and that every sound could be heard. She was playing the piano brought from Germany in the early 1800s, the pride of Holly's mother when she had been alive. Laurette played well, she begrudgingly admitted. She could imagine the two men hanging on every note, watching her. Which one would escort her upstairs?

Holly Beaufort, put thoughts like those out of your head! She flung aside the bed-covers, pushed her feet into slippers, grabbed a robe and went out on to the veranda. The rain had stopped. It was cold, and she hugged the robe high around her neck, but she was glad of it to calm her wandering thoughts. She had other, more important, things to consider. Let Laurette make a fool of herself. When they left, she would be alone again. She would have nothing. Holly would have Tanglewood. She had to be left with Tanglewood! It was her life!

There were fires directly in her line of vision. Fires lighted by the soldiers to keep themselves warm. She had no compassion for them. How dare they tear down her fences and paddock-poles for firewood! Their pleasure was her discomfort. She walked slowly along, staying well away from the iron veranda, where she might be seen from below. She wanted to attract no one from that direction.

'Evening, ma'am.' A cheeky-faced soldier regarded her from a cane chair some feet away, and she came to a sudden, startled, halt. How on earth had he gained access to her private domain? By scaling the ramparts below, obviously. She froze, unsure of herself. How to continue? He was no older than Robert, she thought, and hastily corrected herself. Was, when Robert had been killed, sliced in half by a cannon-shell. Innocent! Too young to die. This Yankee was alive! Animosity triumphed over a natural instinct to feel sorry for the young boy who sat looking at her, his eyes wide. He had a jug of Joseph's corn whiskey in his hand, and she stepped back, realising he was drunk.

'Don't go, ma'am.'

Ma'am! He made her sound like an old maid. She turned and looked back at him, hiding her apprehension. He was no older than she was. What had she to fear?

'Don't you think you should go and get some rest?' she asked in a polite tone. She would not have been so polite had Jared Ruell been in front of her.

'What's the matter? Dirt, am I? Not good enough for your grand company?' The boy staggered to his feet. He was tottering unsteadily as he made his way to where she stood. For a long moment he regarded her without a word, and then the hard expression faded from his face.

'You smell like my sister Suellen. How I miss her. And Mom. My father died at Bull Run. I saw him die. I've never forgotten it. I tried to help him, but I couldn't reach him. I hope she understands.'

'Don't,' Holly said. 'Go and rest. You need rest.'

'You don't want me here, do you? Why? I won't hurt you. I want to talk to someone. Anyone. What's the matter with you damned Southerners? Aren't you human like the rest of us? Don't you mourn your dead?'

He lunged towards her. Whether he was just not steady on his feet or whether he intended to grab her, Holly did not know, but she screamed just the same.

Again and again. It released much of the pent-up emotion which had been building inside her since the arrival of the soldiers. The boy collapsed upon her. She struck at him, threw him off, calling for help at the top of her voice, before realising that there was no one to come to her aid. His friends would consider it amusing that he had got this far. His officers were being entertained by Laurette!

The boy stumbled and fell, catching at her robe as he did so, ripping it from one shoulder. Clutching the torn remnants about her, she ran inside to the sanctuary of her room, and found herself face to face with the sergeant called Wayne.

Old eyes, experienced eyes, disinterested eyes surveyed her, looked past her and encountered the young soldier prostrate on the veranda. He brushed past Holly as though she were invisible, dragged him to his feet and marched him through the room and out of the door before she was aware of what he was doing. Trembling, she sank into a chair and found Mimosa at her side. Where had the girl been all evening? One look into her guilty face told her she had been with Joshua. Holly was too shaken to remonstrate with her.

'Did he touch you?'

Jared Ruell stood in the doorway. How many minutes had passed since the sergeant had taken the unfortunate boy away? She was about to shake her head, and then decided against it. He was at fault. He and his soldiers. No blame could be attached to her. This was her home, not his.

'He was outside.' She met his gaze unflinchingly, and this time the green eyes which encountered his, dark with suspicion, did not falter. 'He—he . . . Look!' She touched her torn robe, her cheeks ashen. 'Ask yourself, Major. What did he come here for?'

Without a word, Jared spun round on his heel and left her. She heard his sharp tones below and they struck terror into her heart. He had said he would hang anyone who went against his orders. She had allowed him to believe the worst—and why not? Why should she care about a Yankee soldier, however young? Young, like Robert. Dear God, she could not allow his inhuman order to be carried out.

Gathering her robe more closely around her, she ran to the head of the stairs, calling after him. There was no answer. No sound from below, but as she reached the bottom of the staircase, Laurette and the lieutenant came out of the sitting-room, arm in arm.

'Holly, are you all right? That dreadful boy!' her sister-in-law began. Her tone was not at all sympathetic. Holly continued on without a word, out through the open doors into the cold night air.

There was a large oak tree in front of the house. Grandfather Lucien had told everyone it had been there when he had first cleared the land to build Tanglewood, and had declared that it was not to be moved. It had grown there in virgin soil from a seedling, and would remain long after his children and grandchildren had departed this world. Holly had agreed with him. The trunk was at least two feet thick in places. The branches, old and gnarled, looked fragile, yet could still hold Joshua's weight. A rope had been thrown over one of them. Beneath it, held by two uniformed soldiers, was the young boy, his face grey with fear. At the sight of her, his face lit up in hope.

'Tell them, ma'am! I meant no harm. I wanted to talk.'

'Talk?' she echoed hollowly, and Jared scrutinised her.

'No more. For the love of God, you know there was

no more to it. I'm drunk. I admit it. Drunk, but not
. . .' His voice trailed off. She was aware of Jared still
watching her. His gaze was unnerving.

'Did he touch you?' he asked again.

'Yes.' It was no more than the truth.

'With rape in mind?' he challenged ruthlessly.

'Yes! No! I don't know.'

'God, Major, she smells sweet like my sister used to.
I just wanted to talk . . .'

'You knew my orders.' At the Major's words, there
came an angry growl from the men about.

'Do you want to see him hang, Miss Beaufort? Damn
your Southern pride. That's all he hurt, isn't it?' Jared
flung the words at her, eyes blazing with contempt. He
did not know if she had deliberately engineered the
event, as her sister-in-law had engineered a fine dinner
and the cosy relaxation afterwards—and he did not care!
His first concern was for one of his men.

'You have left us nothing else. You've taken our men
and killed them, burned our homes, murdered and
plundered your way all through the South, destroying
our way of life. What did we ever do to you?' Holly
asked in a tremulous tone.

'I know this boy, Thompson. He comes from a respectable family. His and mine have been friends for
years. He is head of his now, if he ever goes home. His
father and elder brother are dead. Eighteen years old,
to care for a mother and three sisters. Why not take his
life, if that's the way you feel? Let his mother weep
when she hears the news of his death, as Southern
women have wept over their dead menfolk. As you
wept.' Jared was without mercy. 'Will that satisfy your
desire for revenge?'

'Let him go.' Holly reeled back into the house, sick
at heart. So young! She had almost been the cause of

his death. Were women in the North as vindictive? If they have loved their menfolk, then they were. They could understand her sense of loss. No soldier could! Somehow she contained her tears. Tears now for an enemy? She had not cried for so long, and she would not do so now. Not for a Yankee. Let him have his worthless life. Major Jared Ruell owed her, and she would not allow him to forget it!

Laurette and the lieutenant had returned to the other room, too much interested in each other to care what was going on outside. Holly was filled with disgust at her sister-in-law's behaviour, but she knew it was useless to speak to her further about it. She just did not care. Besides, she was too tired. Her head had been aching for quite a while, and she felt as if the cold that had plagued her for the past week was returning. Honey and lemon spiced with cinnamon was what she needed to make her sleep and to forget what an unpleasant day it had been. She felt suddenly faint as she made her way towards the kitchen. Waves of nausea rose in her stomach and she clutched at a chair for support.

'Miz Holly? Are you all right?' Joseph was standing before her, but she could not see his features clearly. Even as he started anxiously towards her, she slipped to the floor at his feet in a huddle of pink silk.

'Help me, someone!' Joseph called, tentatively touching her hand. It was ice-cold, and her cheeks were like those of a ghost, yet there was a faint film of perspiration on her forehead. Jared Ruell appeared at the door, took in what had happened in a single glance, and wheeled about to call for the doctor before he strode across to them.

'She fainted,' Joseph said in a surprised tone, as the officer bent and lifted Holly up into his arms. 'I've never known her to do that before. Folded like a rag doll right before my eyes.'

'She's feverish.' Jared, too, had seen the unhealthy sheen on her skin. 'Hurry the doctor up, and I'll take her to her room.'

She did not stir as he laid her on the four-poster bed beneath a white muslin canopy and drew a blue patchwork quilt over her. The long golden hair shadowed her face. He bent and gently brushed it away, then quickly straightened as her eyelids quivered, but did not open.

Captain Shaw arrived, took her pulse, and immediately sent Wayne back downstairs to fetch his medical bag. Jared leaned back against the dressing-table, its surface covered with glass trinkets and ladies' toilette requisites. His eyes never left the still figure on the bed. At this moment she looked both fragile and vulnerable, nothing like the defiant young woman who had met him on the porch that morning, and he had to harden his heart against the pity which rose in him. It was not her fault that it was war-time and she was left alone to manage this huge place single-handed. Neither was it his fault that he wore a blue uniform and chose to fight for the Union. They were both victims of circumstance, and must make the best of it.

'Well?' he demanded when the examination was over. Laurette was conspicuous by her absence. He had been right in his assumption that there was no love lost between the two of them. One was a worker, the other a user. She and Rhys were well matched.

'Exhaustion and a slight fever. Her chest is slightly congested. I'll leave her something to clear it up.'

'Can you give her something to make her sleep for the rest of the night? She's had several nasty shocks today, and it would do her good.'

'When I want to take over your command, Jared, I'll ask you to do my job for me,' Shaw growled, searching for his pipe. He turned and caught Joseph's disapproving look behind him, and had second thoughts about it. 'Still, sleep is the natural healer . . . You there, skulking in the doorway!'

Joseph advanced towards the bed, his lined face changing to register indignation at such a summons. Had these Northerners no manners? Even Colonel Beaufort had never used such a tone with him. Skulking, indeed!

'Give your mistress these two pills when she recovers, which should be any minute now. Make her take them with some warm milk, and don't let anyone disturb her until late tomorrow morning. Does that meet with your approval, Major?'

Jared straightened up, with a nod. Despite the way they talked to each other, they were old friends, and Shaw was the best army doctor he had come across. Again, an old campaigner from the Indian wars of the 1850s.

'Come on, you crusty old devil. I've some fine brandy downstairs that you may appreciate. And if that's too smooth for your jaded palate, Wayne has uncovered several jugs of corn whiskey.'

He preceded the doctor through the door without looking back at the bed. He did not want to look at Holly again or remember the softness of her against him as he carried her upstairs. The sweet fragrance of her hair, soft as silk against his hands. She had become far more of a danger to him than she could ever imagine. A desirable enemy. He had to remember only the latter. The enemy. There was no place for her in his life, nor for him in hers.

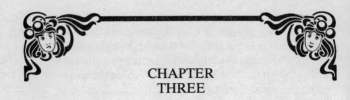

CHAPTER
THREE

HOLLY AWOKE to find the sun streaming through the partly drawn blue chintz curtains at the windows. How lovely to see it again after days of rain and overcast skies, she thought, stretching languidly. How relaxed she felt, and then her eyes fell on the small china-encased clock on the dressing-table and she started up in horror. Twelve-thirty! It was impossible. She had never slept this late before. The clock must have stopped in the night.

It had not, she discovered when she climbed out of bed and checked it. She had overslept. It could only have been the milk Mimosa gave her. What on earth had been in it? Certainly not one of cook's herbal remedies; they did not work so efficiently. Neither had the medicine she had taken before the milk contained anything able to induce such sleep. It had reminded her of the sweet-tasting remedies her mother had once made. Perfectly harmless.

'Mimosa, what did you put in my milk last night?' she demanded, going straight to the kitchen the moment she was dressed.

The girl looked at her guiltily, confirming her suspicions.

'Only some white powder Joseph ground up, Miz Holly. He said you wouldn't take no tablets if you knew they came from the Yankee doctor.'

'How right he was,' Holly began indignantly, but then

her anger subsided. She did feel better, and she had not begun to cough as she usually did each morning after getting out of bed. 'Where is Joseph? The house is like a graveyard this morning.'

'Out with that Major. Getting chickens for dinner. I heard something about you all eating together. Miz Laurette arranged it. Best silver, best china, best everything, she said. Is that all right, Miz Holly?'

'It is not! We have to suffer them being here, but we are not going to make them welcome, or too comfortable. The Willow Pattern will do for them, and please hide some of father's brandy, if it isn't too late—and his cigars—or he will have nothing to come back to. Did you put away those grain-sacks with Joshua as I ordered?'

'Yes, Miz Holly. Buried deep under the lightning-tree behind the paddocks. No one find them there.'

'Good girl.' Holly turned away with a smile. Laurette might have capitulated, but she never would.

Her sister-in-law came into the house at the side of Jared Ruell as Holly turned to go back upstairs to fetch a coat before she went out. She was laughing at something he had said, her pretty face upturned towards his, her eyelids fluttering coyly. That was better saved for the lieutenant, she thought, noticing that Jared's attention was elsewhere.

'Miss Beaufort, I'm glad to see you are feeling no ill-effects after the unfortunate incident last night.' He stopped a few paces from her, and inclined his head in a polite nod. 'Mrs Beaufort felt sure you would have recovered sufficiently to dine with us tonight.'

'She was wrong, Major. I have no intention of doing so. I shall be eating in my room as I did last night, and shall continue to do, until you leave.'

'Holly Beaufort, how can you be so rude to our guests?' Laurette demanded in a peeved tone.

'Guests? Guests are invited. I did not invite Yankee soldiers beneath my roof,' Holly snapped. 'Our laws of hospitality, great as they are, do not, in my book, extend to accommodating the enemy.'

'Or to being civil.' Jared's gaze was cold. 'That's a pity, as it would make things so much easier for all of us. Have it your own way. You will come downstairs tonight, Miss Beaufort, and you will conduct yourself in a manner more suitable to your station, or I may feel inclined to turn you over my knee and soundly spank you. If you act like a naughty little girl, I shall treat you like one. And if you are not down here by eight o'clock I shall send Sergeant Wayne to fetch you, and his manners, at times, leave a great deal to be desired. You would not like that side of him at all.'

'You—you would not dare,' Holly gasped, her cheeks flushing bright pink at the threat. Laurette giggled behind a gloved hand, and she glared at her, fuming at her helplessness.

'Try me,' Jared suggested, and continued on into the sitting-room.

'You asked for that,' Laurette said quietly, drawing her shawl closer round her shoulders. 'He's man enough to do it, too. You've met your match this time, Holly.'

The bright sunshine which met Holly as she stepped outside did nothing to dispel her despondent mood. The nerve of that man! Spank her? He would, too, she knew it. He was an unfeeling brute. Not for one minute did she consider the fact that she had deserved the reprimand, that she had been ruder to him than to anyone else in all her twenty years. She could not bear the thought of spending the whole evening in his loathsome presence, watching Laurette make eyes at Lieutenant Rhys. Was he expecting her to act in the same coquettish manner? Was that the reason he had issued such an ultimatum, or was it his intention to humiliate her still further in some way yet unknown to her? She would not go. She would lock herself in her room!

She spent an hour talking with Joshua in one of the sheds. They had to find a way to secrete some of the precious sacks of grain and seed before the Yankees laid their greedy hands on them, but, as the negro said, it was not easy to do anything under the noses of thirty troopers. He and Mimosa had, so far, put six sacks out of reach, the last three the night before in pitch darkness, and that managed only with the help of some of the women who had kept the soldiers occupied.

'Thank them for me,' Holly said warmly.

'It won't be necessary. They know their own future, too, depends on those food sacks. They did it as much for themselves as for you,' Joshua returned off-handedly.

She left him to return to his work and went back to the house to try and finish the ledgers. A dozen or more troopers, led by Lieutenant Rhys, rode past her as she mounted the veranda steps, and she felt herself grow cold with fear as she contemplated where they might be going.

There was not another plantation close at hand, but there were several small places, farms and small-holdings. Most of them also had slaves, and the land was still rich with unpicked fruit and vegetables in abundance. If only she had some way of warning her neighbours. It would be days before they could get round to them all.

She became aware of a uniformed figure watching her from the far end of the veranda and, looking up, found Jared's gaze full on her. Frightened lest she had given away her concern, she hurried inside and shut herself in the study.

She heard the soldiers return as it was growing dark, and ran to the window to watch them. They had extra horses with them, mares and small foals. They had raided the Dickinson place, she thought, horrified. Her father bought all his horses there, for it was the best stud farm in the country, run now by Mrs Dickinson, who was in her sixties. Her husband had been dead many years. Since the war began, she had lost a son and a grandson, barely eighteen. Those awful, awful men, she thought, turning back into the room, her face full of disgust. One old woman and a couple of farm hands. What kind of a fight could she have put up? Her prize stock confiscated. What had happened to her, and to the house?

Somehow Holly stopped herself from rushing out to confront Major Ruell. He had sent the men out. He knew exactly what they were in for. But she had to know. Waiting for a moment to compose herself, she went in search of Mimosa and ordered her to prepare a hot bath and then lay out clothes for that evening.

'Lordy, Miz Holly, you ain't eatin' with them, too, are you?' The girl looked at her in surprise. 'This morning you said . . .'

'Mimosa, are you happy here?' Holly fixed her with a stern look.

'Yes, Miz Holly. You know I am.'

'Then hold your tongue, unless you want me to send you packing with the rest of those no-account darkies who think the soldiers are going to give them a better life than they have here. I want you upstairs in ten minutes, do you hear?'

She rarely raised her voice with any of the servants, or indeed had cause to issue threats. She was well liked and generally respected. Mimosa, deciding something was very wrong, nodded vigorously and scampered towards the kitchen to heat water for the bath.

From the window of her room, Holly looked out at the lawns and flower-beds, and her heart ached at the sight of the tents and camp-fires which littered the whole area in front of the house. The soldiers had no respect for property. So much for the orders of their commanding officer. If this was the way they acted now, how would it be when they left, she thought with mounting anxiety. The house was full of priceless pictures and rare pieces of French furniture, not to mention the collection of her mother's and grandmother's jewellery, which was irreplaceable. She would shoot any soldier she caught stealing, she thought boldly, and then remembered the single bullet in the Derringer. No, she would save that for Major Jared Ruell if he allowed his men to rampage unchallenged through the house. No one, she vowed, was going to strip Tanglewood of the heritage left to it by grandfather Lucien. The house and its contents was a monument to his courage and that of his wife, to be cherished and loved by future generations of Beauforts—and to be protected at all costs.

She turned and looked at the two dresses spread out on the bed. One was of dark green velvet, the other of yellow watered silk, embroidered with tiny flowers. It had been made for her nineteenth birthday, but since the outbreak of war had taken brothers and father far away, the dress had been returned to the closet unworn. No! She would not wear that to charm Jared Ruell. It was to welcome her father back home. The green suited her well enough.

Mimosa helped her into it without a word. The girl had hardly spoken since that morning, and Holly felt remorse for her sharp words. She smiled as she studied herself in the mirror. It felt good to wear a pretty dress again. She was growing too used to her old skirts and worn blouses. Most of her good day-dresses had been cut up long ago to make work-clothes. All that remained in her closet now were four out-of-date ball-gowns, the green, the yellow, and several rather severely styled dresses which she kept for formal occasions or funerals. She had not been able to buy a new bolt of cloth in over a year, thanks to the Yankee blockade of Southern ports. Pins and thread were scarce, too, which meant that alterations had to be kept to a minimum. Hair ribbon was almost non-existent.

Mimosa piled the well-brushed curls on the top of Holly's head, and secured them with two combs adorned with tiny seed-pearls.

'You look right pretty, Miz Holly. Can't remember the last time you dressed up this way.'

'No more can I. Perhaps it will do me good. I won't need you any more tonight, Mimosa. Run along and have something to eat with Joshua in the kitchen.'

'Thank you, Miz Holly. Don't you worry none about those two Yankees tonight. Joshua says he won't leave the house until they are back in their rooms.'

'You tell him to stay well out of sight,' Holly warned. 'I want no heroics from anyone.'

Mimosa gave her a secretive smile, as though to indicate that she knew something of importance, but was gone before Holly could question her further. With a sigh she took a last look at her reflection in the gilt-framed wall mirror. All this on the orders of a Yankee major. *Holly Beaufort, you should be ashamed of yourself.* He would believe he had frightened her with his threats. Well, let him. She desperately needed news of the war, and he or his lieutenant would supply it. She intended to make sure her evening was not totally wasted.

'Holly, my dear, I declare you look quite ravishing. Does she not, gentlemen?' Laurette looked at the elegantly groomed young woman who entered the sitting-room where she and the two officers were enjoying a before-dinner drink. 'How that colour does suit you. That is the dress you wore the night of your engagement party, wasn't it?'

'How clever of you to remember,' Holly returned in a honeyed tone, accepting the glass of red wine Joseph brought to her on a silver tray. His face was inscrutable. She hoped he would understand why she had changed her mind and decided to come downstairs. She had forgotten that night, over four years ago now, when she had become engaged to Richard Mitchell. She had all but forgotten what he looked like, too, the stranger whom Clayton had brought to the house the first time Laurette came to visit. Who, in the months which followed, had charmed her, an unworldly fifteen-year-old. They had become engaged on her sixteenth birthday, and four months later he went off to war. At first the letters had been quick to come, then less frequent, until they stopped altogether. For a year she had not known whether he was alive or dead. During that time, when she had nothing else to do but think about the war and what it meant to all of them, she realised that Richard hardly came into her future plans. He had been a smooth-tongued charmer, but there had been no substance to him. The infatuation had ended as quickly as it had begun, and she had realised that the war had saved her from a disastrous and probably very unhappy marriage.

'Holly's fiancé is in Virginia. A captain,' Laurette went on. What had prompted her to mention Richard

now, Holly wondered. And how did she know he was
a captain. She did not. She had heard that both he and
her father were in Savannah last December, and had
journeyed there to see them, hoping to explain her
change of heart to Richard. It was a cruel thing to do,
but better than waiting for him to return and then telling
him that what she had taken for love was nothing more
than a summer romance, not meant to endure. But he
had moved on, and instead she had found Laurette,
resting in the city before making her way to Tanglewood.

Holly had not thought to question her presence there
until afterwards, when she began to wonder—why Savannah, when Laurette had left her father's farm after
Clayton's death in September, and the property lay just
outside Atlanta? Where had she been for those missing
months? She had never asked. Laurette's miscarriage
and later illness had wiped all questions from her mind.
Now they came crowding back and there was no answer
she found satisfying.

'Miss Beaufort, I am glad you accepted my invitation.'
Jared Ruell stood before her, took the hand she extended somewhat haughtily towards him, and laid his
lips against her fingers. 'I promise that tonight I shall
have all the chivalry of a Southern gentleman,' he added
in a lower tone, and she snatched her hand free.

'This house is accustomed only to gentlemen,' Holly
answered, and moved past him to a chair beside the
fire.

Tim Rhys nodded his head in her direction, but did
not get up. Joshua had more manners, she thought,
ignoring him, and he could not read or write!

'Dinner will be ready in ten minutes,' Joseph said
quietly before he left the room, and Holly silently sighed
with relief. She felt awkward and ill at ease in the

present company, and all the questions so carefully prepared while she was upstairs had vanished from her mind.

Jared replenished his empty glass with wine. She shook her head when he looked significantly at her half-full glass. He came and stood at her side and she became aware, as on the first occasion when their eyes had met, of the magnetism radiating from him. Her breath caught in her throat as she again encountered his grey eyes. Tonight they were more friendly than ever before, unshadowed by either suspicion or tiredness. As he studied her face in silence, she began to feel a flush of embarrassed colour stealing into her cheeks and, at the sight of it, a soft laugh broke from his lips.

'How pleasant to discover a woman who can still blush.'

'I am not accustomed to being stared at so rudely, Major.' She was horrified to find her voice unsteady.

'I was thinking what a lucky man your fiancé is, having you to come back to,' Jared remarked gently. As she stared at him in surprise, he added, 'Did I not tell you I would be civil tonight? I cannot see why it is necessary for us to be at each other's throats. Can you? Apart from my uniform, that is.'

Complacent devil! Holly thought, fighting down a sarcastic retort. She drank her wine and held out the glass, forcing a smile to her stiff lips.

'You are right, of course. I should make the best of what cannot be avoided. May I have a little more wine, please, Major. It has been a long time since I have had a chance to sit and talk to anyone. You will sit beside me at dinner, I hope, and tell me all the news which passes us by here. Sometimes I have thought it was better that way, but there are times when I have regretted our ignorant state.'

As he moved away, she saw Laurette's narrowed gaze on her. Let her think what she liked! Holly's reasons were beyond reproach. She had not sought the company of Jared Ruell. He had sought hers, and he was making it easy to forget who and what he was tonight. How those eyes of his constantly changed. Pale grey, disturbing in their intensity. Dark, like gathering storm-clouds, screening his thoughts from her. He was handsome, she admitted reluctantly, as he returned to her side. He wore his uniform with an air of a man born to command. Did he have a home and family waiting somewhere for him to return to? Children and a wife who would mourn him if he was killed? He must have, he was too good looking to.have remained a bachelor.

They sat side by side at dinner, opposite Laurette and the lieutenant, who further exhibited his exceptional lack of manners by lounging over the table as he slurped noisily at the turkey soup and insisted on drinking brandy when Joseph served wine to everyone else. It was as if he wanted to shock her, Holly thought, turning from him. It was for one night only and soon they would be gone. She must do and say nothing to jeopardise the future of her home, herself or the slaves who remained loyal and would be staying on after the soldiers had gone. It was an effort, but she would do it!

On the other hand, Jared's behaviour was impeccable. Holly could fault him on nothing. He complimented her on the food and asked if he could have the recipe for the roast ham which arrived, dripping with butter and honey and surrounded by yams and baked potatoes. There were side plates of freshly cooked rolls, winter peas and crisp bacon. Although she enjoyed every mouthful, Holly could not help wishing Laurette had not been so generous with their precious supplies.

Besides, she was giving the Yankees a false impression of wealth and gracious living with such a spread. They did not eat like this every day!

To follow, cook had prepared a rich chocolate sponge, sandwiched together with cream and strawberry jam, and peaches pickled in brandy. Afterwards Joseph served steaming hot coffee in the silver pot that had belonged to Holly's grandmother, pouring it into Wedgwood bone china cups.

'Shall we take this through into the other room? I am sure you gentlemen would like brandy and cigars with it.' Holly asked, pushing back her chair.

The evening was less of a strain than she had expected, but her enjoyment had been marred by the war news Jared had given her. He made no bones about his opinion that the South had lost the war and should capitulate unconditionally to save further waste of lives and property. In her heart of hearts she agreed with him, but she would never have admitted it out loud. He spoke of Sherman's total victory in Georgia and of his plans to march on to Columbia. Charleston would also fall soon, he speculated, and that left North Carolina and Virginia, where the Union armies of all commands would meet to take Richmond.

Holly stayed silent, visualising the blood-baths to come, the tattered remnants of the Confederacy mustered against well-disciplined, well-armed veterans from the North. Yes, the war was lost for the South. Why, of why, did someone not stop it now? She learned that Robert E. Lee had become Commander-in-Chief of all the Confederate armies. The greatest leader they had, in her estimation. Would he stop the senseless slaughter before the South was deprived of more men and boys? If he did not, there would soon be only women and children and the very old left to start again when the chaos was over. Start what? Many had nothing to begin a new life with.

'Have you seen any of your family since the war began?' Jared asked, seating himself beside her on the velvet-covered chesterfield beside the fire.

'My father, last December. For two whole hours in Savannah. I had not seen him for two and a half years. Richard, my fiancé, had left the day before. I have not seen him since the outbreak of war when he volunteered.' Now why had she mentioned him, Holly wondered? As protection against the man beside her? A wedge to keep them apart, to stop her from liking him too much? She did not like him. She was being civil to him out of necessity, and that was not the same thing. She was lonely and it was nice to talk to someone—anyone. It meant nothing! How hard she was trying to convince herself that the strange feeling inside her did not presage attraction. 'My brother Robert was killed at the first battle of Bull Run. Clayton, Laurette's husband, as I told you, died defending Atlanta. How have you fared in this war, Major?'

There was bitterness in her voice and in the expressive green eyes she lowered over her coffee, and, for at least the tenth time that evening, he cursed that the subject of the war had ever been introduced to the conversation. But that was all she had been interested in. He had realised from the beginning she wanted only to reassure herself of the safety and well-being of the last two people left to her. He had not been able to give her those assurances. He could only give her the facts of what was to happen, but no hope.

What had he expected from the evening, he wondered? He came to the conclusion that he preferred Holly Beaufort spitting fire and insults at him; that way, he knew where he was. The woman sitting close beside him, the fragrance of a sweet perfume wafting between them, the green velvet enhancing the rich golden curls on the crown of her head, was the nearest thing to an angel he was ever likely to encounter in his lifetime. But was she real or an illusion? Women were fickle creatures, deceptive, with more sides to them than a highly-polished diamond. Here she was, a picture of perfection, all smiles and honeyed tones, yet this morning she had flatly refused to dine with him. He was not stupid enough to believe that his threat to send Wayne to fetch her from her room had changed her mind. Then what had? Unless she had decided to play the same game as her sister-in-law? Maybe the show of animosity had been a sham. Could he have been so wrong about her?

'My father was in the Mexican wars and too old for this one, thank God. My brother runs the family business. He thinks wars are a waste of time, against the laws of God and man. He, too, stayed out of it.'

'If there were more like him, perhaps there never would have been a war and we would have been left in peace to run our lives as we see fit,' Holly said, looking up. 'Who are you to tell us what is right or wrong? You know nothing about us or our way of life—a way of life you have destroyed.'

'Holly, hush! My, how you do carry on,' Laurette reproved with a shaky laugh, as though she suspected Holly might be tiring of the man at her side and about to let loose a tirade of abuse and condemnation. Things were going too nicely with her for the moment to have them spoiled. 'Here's Joseph with the brandy. Well, what have we here?'

Following in Joseph's footsteps came a young soldier, another tray of coffee in his hands. Holly's eyes widened as she recognised the boy who had nearly been hanged because of her.

'Thompson was feeling quite ashamed of himself this morning,' Jared said calmly, accepting a glass of brandy and a cigar from the silver box Joseph held out. 'And as your man told me how short-handed you were, I thought he might lend a hand wherever needed. Isn't that so, Private Thompson?'

'Yes, sir.' Beetroot red, the boy nodded. He looked neither at Holly nor in the direction of the lieutenant and Laurette as he set down the tray and backed hurriedly towards the door. 'Will that be all, Mr Joseph?'

'That's all, boy. You get back to the kitchen now, cook's waiting for you,' Joseph said without looking around. Holly had taken a glass of brandy. The first time in her life she had ever touched spirits, that he could recall. What was the girl going to do next?

'I think I feel almost sorry for him,' she murmured, and Jared looked at her questioningly.

'Why? After what he tried to do to you? No punishment, short of death, is too great, surely?'

'Don't make fun of me, Major.' Her tone sharpened at his jibe. 'I suppose you think me very foolish for acting as I did last night, but I was very frightened. Everything happened so quickly. I over-reacted . . .'

'I also regret the event.' The way he spoke, he sounded as though he half blamed her for what had almost happened, but there was nothing in his expression to confirm the suspicion. 'The boy over-reacted, as you put it, too. His was an over-reaction to war and the gruesome sights he has seen and tried to forget since he enlisted. The whiskey deadened his fears, the nightmare thoughts. I think he just wanted to talk to someone. Surely you must know what that feels like?'

'You are very perceptive.' She wished he were not. Much as she wanted to open her heart to someone, it could not—must not—be to him.

'And you are very alone.' Jared spoke to her ears only, aware of a growing uneasiness about her. Was she growing tired of the game already? Beautiful, lonely—and available? Was that the real Holly Beaufort? He went to take a drink and saw that he had already emptied his glass without realising it.

As a frown creased his face, Holly became aware of something that she was at a loss to understand. For a moment, as he regarded her from the top of her shining curls to the hem of the green dress which so beautifully complemented her eyes, she felt as if the couch moved beneath her. Neither Laurette nor her companion existed. Time stood still. No one had ever looked at her in this way, desiring her with his eyes without a single word being spoken. She had had many admirers before the war, even after her engagement to Richard, but they had been adolescent attractions, quickly forgotten. Even the love she had thought she had found for Richard had been a myth. He had never looked at her like this. She would have been shocked if he had—then. In four years she had grown up considerably. No longer shocked, but frightened by the open invitation Jared Ruell seemed to be extending. In the space of a heartbeat he had become different, and she did not like it.

Putting aside her brandy, untouched, she rose to her feet, knowing that she must leave the room before her silence was taken as an acceptance of his offer. She was not Laurette! How dare he regard her in the same light as her wanton sister-in-law, who sat watching her with an amused smile, her manner openly proclaiming that she cared nothing what people thought of her. She no longer had any standards, any morals, Holly thought, horrified, and shut her mind to how far Laurette was prepared to go in order to secure a future for the morrow. Was she too blind to realise that Rhys was no better, and could not be trusted any more than Jared Ruell, his commanding officer? The man who had sent soldiers out that very morning to lay waste to the home of an old woman and steal her livelihood and then sat and ate with them, acting the gentleman, as if nothing had happened. They had the blood of innocent men and women on their hands. She must have been mad to give in so easily.

'I am rather tired, Major, I think I will retire. Please stay and have some more brandy. Lieutenant, I am sure Laurette will see you are well cared for.'

Somehow she smiled as she said good-night, but the moment the door closed behind her, her cheeks blanched and she passed a hand shakily over her forehead. Dear God, please make them go soon, she prayed, hurrying towards the staircase. Without knowing why, she was suddenly very much afraid.

Jared Ruell moved so swiftly and quietly that she was not aware of him behind her until she was at the door of her room. The hand laid on her arm from behind brought her spinning round, a half-scream rising in her throat—which she stifled, a hand against her mouth at the sight of his tall frame. She had not realised before how tall he was. In the shadowed corridor he dwarfed her. She felt somehow threatened!

'I didn't startle you, surely?' he enquired softly. 'You were expecting me, were you not?' His voice was all velvety softness, yet somehow menacing.

'No! Whatever gave you that idea, Major Ruell?' she demanded, removing his hand with great dignity when he made no attempt to do so. 'Why have you followed me? What have you to say that could not be said openly downstairs? Not an apology for your intrusion into my home, surely?'

She was tired of being polite, and her voice was as sharp as it had been to him that morning. In the semi-darkness Jared's features creased into a smile.

'Of course you expected it. Isn't that what all this finery and polite conversation has been about tonight? I have received treatment I'm sure is kept only for your Southern gentlemen, and there has to be a good reason. Wasn't it meant as an invitation? Your sister-in-law certainly meant it as one. That's why my lieutenant will be in her bed tonight, exactly as she hoped.' Holly gasped as if he had struck her, and tried to open the door of her room, but his hands imprisoned her wrists. 'When someone throws a challenge in my face, Miss Beaufort,' he continued, his fingers biting into her soft skin until she winced in pain. 'I take them up on it.'

She opened her mouth to call for Joseph, but no sound was ever uttered. It was smothered beneath the mouth which ground into hers, shocking her into silence. She fought in vain to free herself, tried to twist her head and free her lips, but she was a child in his grasp. He kissed her as if he hated her, she thought, her senses reeling under the assault which rendered her incapable of thinking clearly.

Richard had kissed her quite ardently the night before he went away, and she had run indoors, both upset and puzzled by the change in his attitude which had turned him from a considerate young man, always courteous, ever careful never to offend her in the slightest way, into an insistant lover who wanted more from her than the usual kiss and permitted embraces. She had put it down to the fact that they would be parted for some considerable time, but his lack of letters had made her wonder. She felt guilty about the mistake she had almost made, but was there any need? Perhaps he had found someone else to interest him while he was away.

Jared Ruell's kisses had the same unreasonable urgency about them. Almost desperation. She was just thinking she would faint if he did not release her, when his arms slackened and fell away and she stepped back from him, wiping a hand across her mouth in a gesture of disgust.

'How—how dare you!' She wanted to say much more, but was so full of rage, of humiliation, that no words would come.

'Perhaps I did mistake the signals after all,' Jared said in a strange tone. 'You're a child playing at being a woman. No, not even that. You don't know what you are, any more. You look all woman, but you think and act like a man. Half of me respects your courage, the other half pities what you are missing.'

'What the war has taken from me,' Holly blazed. Did he not think she missed those past days, her family around her, the peace, the love she had known in this old house? She had none of those things now, only memories, and memories did not keep food on the table, produce cotton in the fields, or run a plantation. 'What men like you have taken from me!'

'So I am solely to blame, am I? I suppose you have to have someone you can use to appease your hurt pride, to blame for the loss of your womanhood. But if I have taken, I can also give.' His voice became soft again, terribly mocking in its softness. 'Do you want to feel like a woman, Holly Beaufort? If you do, I am at your service. I am sure you will find me an apt teacher. As apt, I suspect, as you would be a pupil.'

The sound of the slap Holly dealt him hung heavily

in the air between them. She had hit him so hard that her hand hurt.

'You're a high-spirited little filly underneath that air of "I don't give a damn", aren't you? Be careful. You won't get any soft-glove treatment from me,' he drawled, indifferent to her indignation.

'Then we know exactly where we both stand, don't we,' Holly retorted, fingers stealing to the doorknob. She heard him chuckle as she stepped quickly inside, slammed the door and turned the key in the lock. With her back against it, she heard his footsteps fade as he went into his own room. Picking up her skirts, she fled into her sitting-room and made sure that its door was also locked. From her side, she could hear the sound of whistling. Trembling, she sank down into a chair without bothering to light a lamp. Thank goodness she had not asked Mimosa to wait up for her—she wanted no one to see the state she was in. She was shaking like an aspen-leaf, could hardly breathe. Her lips felt bruised, her wrists, too. As she sat in the darkness, allowing her composure to return slowly, shutting her ears to the sound of movement from the other room, the infuriating whistling that continued incessantly, one question—one unanswerable question— came again and again into her troubled mind. She hated Jared Ruell and everything he stood for. Why then, in that second before he released her, had her traitorous lips softened beneath his?

CHAPTER
FOUR

'GOING SOMEWHERE, Miss Beaufort?'

Holly's head flew up with a gasp of annoyance as the voice of Lieutenant Rhys sounded from the stable doorway. She had slipped out of the house before seven and ordered the groom to saddle her horse in the hope that she could ride away from Tanglewood unnoticed. She had to find out if Mrs Dickinson was all right.

'I may be. What business is it of yours?' she replied coldly. Whereas earlier his bold gaze had embarrassed her, it now served to remind her of the previous night, and fresh anger surged through her as she remembered Jared Ruell's arms about her, his lips grinding cruelly into hers. The guilt which seized her each time she recalled that fleeting moment, when his kiss had evoked a response from her, intensified the anger and her loathing of both men. 'Continue with what you are doing,' she ordered the negro lad who paused in the act of tightening the saddle girth around her mare. She was riding out if she had to go over him.

'You have permission from the Major?'

'Would I be here otherwise?' she lied, not a tremor in her voice.

To her horror, the man threw back his head and laughed aloud. The sound grated on her nerves, but she managed to retain her composure and motioned to the groom to hurry and finish what he was doing.

'In a good mood, is he? Enjoyed his evening, no

doubt?' He knew Jared Ruell had followed her! Her cheeks flamed, and she was about to deny his surmise that they had spent the night together. But she changed her mind, believing that he would not question her leaving the house unchaperoned—at least she hoped not. Had they discussed how each would act, before the two women arrived to join them? Between themselves, men were supposed to boast of their exploits. Soldiers, she suspected, would be the worst culprits, being able to engage in all manner of illicit affairs and partnerships while far away from home, and their poor wives would never know. 'These little diversions have alleviated a great deal of boredom, especially while we were coming through Georgia. And not only for me,' he added meaningly.

'You have a sick mind,' Holly said disgustedly. What he was suggesting was too humiliating to contemplate. Lonely women, young girls, alone and helpless under the yoke of an enemy army, at the mercy of men like the lieutenant who considered them easy game and of no consequence. Not even worth a second thought. Was that how he thought of Laurette?

'Is—is my sister-in-law one of your diversions, Lieutenant?'

'A very accommodating one,' Rhys said, his rather thin face breaking into a smile as he considered the relationship he now shared with the other girl. 'She has an insatiable appetite, that one. She will never be without a man for long. She would never survive.'

'You are disgusting!'

'You are no different. If you've got the Major eating out of your hand this morning, you must have had your work cut out. Although he has a way with him, I must admit. He's usually very successful with that quiet charm of his, and a sympathetic manner works every time with a lonely woman. And your man has been away a long time, hasn't he, Miss Beaufort?'

'Lieutenant Rhys, the Major would like to see you, sir, before you go out on patrol.' Sergeant Wayne appeared behind him. Holly wondered if he had overheard any of their conversation, and quickly mounted her horse, anxious to be gone from the presence of them both.

'Are you going out, miss?' Wayne asked, stepping in front of her as she turned the mount towards him.

'Yes, Sergeant. Unlike your men, who seem able to lounge around here all day, stealing my chickens and anything else they can lay their hands on, and filling the heads of my negroes with their stupid talk of freedom and streets back North paved with gold and just waiting for the black man to walk along, I have a plantation to run. Your Major Ruell has given me permission to go out. Ask him if you don't believe me.'

'I shall, miss. Wait here until I come back.' Wayne spun on his heel. She knew he did not believe her.

'Of course she has his permission,' the lieutenant said, throwing Holly a knowing look before he turned and followed him. 'They were together last night, weren't they?'

Holly waited until they reached the steps of the veranda before edging her horse into the doorway. The moment they disappeared inside, she dug her heels into the animal's flanks and she leapt away towards the paddocks, almost colliding with one of the troop cooks who had just raided the hen-house. The bowl of fresh eggs he carried shot into the air, seemed to hover for an instant, and then descended rapidly on to his head and shoulders, covering him with bright yellow yolks. The soldiers would not have those for breakfast, Holly thought triumphantly as she kneed the bay mare and she went up and over the top gate, all of six feet in height, and galloped swiftly towards the fields.

How many times had she ridden this way with her brothers, outriding both of them most times. Only her father ever beat her. He was a magnificent horseman. Where was he now? She closed her mind against that train of thought. Until news came of his whereabouts, it was best to think of other things.

She reined in abruptly to gather her bearings, and heard shouting behind her. She looked back and could just make out a crowd of uniformed figures surrounding the pathetic, sticky apparition of the cook. Her eyes sparkled with pure pleasure at the mischief she had unwittingly caused. The group broke and ran in all directions. The smile vanished from her face as a horseman appeared from the midst of them. The lieutenant, learning that she had no permission, was coming after her! Horse and rider cleared the top paddock gate without effort. He was a good horseman, she realised, glancing frantically back. Which direction? She could not go to the Dickinson farm until she had lost him. Not for one moment did she think he would catch her. Her horse was the fastest in the stables, and she groomed and cared for her personally. Clayton had given her the mare the Christmas before he went away.

Wheeling away to the right, she skirted the slave cabins at a fierce gallop, throwing up mud and earth in her headlong flight. Men and women looked up from their work to watch her pass, or moved aside to avoid being plastered with reddish-brown ooze. Curious eyes first watched her progress until she was gone from sight into the pine-trees which extended in a thin belt a mile long, ending at the edge of the family graveyard, then swivelled to stare at the horseman who rode at a similar reckless pace after her. There were a few shoulders shrugged as duties were resumed. It was not their place to wonder what was happening, or to voice comment.

Holly slowed her mount and looked behind her. She could see no signs of pursuit, but she could hear it. The drumming of hooves not far to her rear, and the screeching and flight of some wild birds as they took to the air in panic, were indications that he was rapidly gaining on her. Desperately she gave the mare her head and galloped in the direction of the river. There were hundreds of places along the bank where swamp grass grew thick and high, and gnarled old trees had dominated the scene long before Tanglewood came into existence. One could hide in their hollowed trunks, which were big enough sometimes to contain both a rider and a horse.

It had not rained the night before, but the ground was still soft and treacherous, and more than once Holly was almost thrown headlong from the saddle as the animal slithered on soft mud. She had to make the river. She was almost there. Another few minutes and her rapidly tiring horse could rest. When the lieutenant had given up searching for her, she would continue on to the Dickinson place. Mrs Dickinson would be offered a home at Tanglewood, Holly decided. It was unthinkable for her to remain alone and unprotected under these circumstances.

A horseman came careering out of the trees to her left, veered across her path and forced her to pull up sharply to avoid a collision. Before she could gather her scattered wits, Jared Ruell had grabbed the reins from her hands, leapt to the ground and pulled her bodily from the saddle. She could not believe it! He had pursued her! With clenched fists, she struck at his face. With an oath, he caught both her wrists in one hand, fastened the other in the loose curls at the nape of her neck and jerked back her head.

'Behave yourself, or I'll knock you cold and take you back across your saddle,' he threatened.

It was partly the threat, which she knew instinctively he would not hesitate to carry out, and also the pain of his fingers entwined in her hair that forced her to obey.

'That's better,' Jared snapped, his eyes blazing with anger, like sparks off a polished blade in the heat of a forge.

'You!' Holly sagged weakly in his grasp, still unable to comprehend why he had chased her instead of sending troopers or the lieutenant.

'Who did you think it was? Rhys? No, I couldn't send him, he'd have enjoyed the chase too much, and what I suspect he had in mind for you afterwards,' came the chilling answer.

'Afterwards?' Holly stammered.

'You lied to him and I reprimanded him for believing you. He doesn't like to be made to look a fool, even if he is one. You would not have liked the penalty he intended to exact for that little piece of trickery. Had I sent my sergeant, he would have ridden you into the ground and then dragged you back on the end of a rope for wasting my time and his!'

'And you, Major?' Holly asked in a contemptuous tone. She sounded so brave, but inside she was shaking with fear and apprehension. 'What punishment have you devised for me?'

Jared eased his hold on her hair slightly as he stared down into the defiant features, and the smile which creased his face told her he knew what was in her heart.

'Maybe I should haul you over to the Dickinson place. That's where you were heading, isn't it?' He felt her tense in his grasp as he delivered the words without mercy.

'What have you done?' she whispered, appalled. What would she have found?

He was silent. As she waited breathlessly for an answer, she watched a slow flush steal over his skin. His mouth tightening, Jared released her and swung away. He said harshly, 'Rhys exceeded his orders. He was attacked, and he retaliated, but to excess. Several men were killed and the house destroyed. I am filing charges against him as soon as I catch up with the main force.'

'Mrs Dickinson?' Holly's tone was almost inaudible. She was shaking now, but whether from the cold wind which was sweeping across from the river, or from the dread in her heart as she visualised the terrible outcome of the lieutenant's excesses, she did not know.

'Alive, but shaken, as you can imagine. She was harbouring two rebel soldiers in one of her bars. They refused to surrender, and Rhys ordered his men to open fire. Afterwards he burnt the house, destroyed everything which could have been of use to the enemy, before returning. Sergeant Wayne has gone back there this morning with half a dozen men. They are going to salvage what they can for the old woman and then she is to be escorted to Savannah, where she has relatives. Damn it, this is war!' he ejaculated as Holly covered her eyes with her hands. 'She knew what she was doing when she hid them.'

'She has lost a son and a grandson already. Now you have taken her home, too. You have left her nothing. Lieutenant Rhys may have given the orders then, but you sent him out,' she accused bitterly. 'What orders did you give him?'

That no house remain standing that can offer shelter to the enemy, no food be available that could sustain them and so prolong their fighting ability and, in turn, the war. Treat any Southerner—man, woman or child—who

*offers resistance or takes up a weapon against a blue
uniform as an enemy, and deal with them accordingly.*
Jared remembered his orders as vividly as though he
had only just received them. His commanding officer
had been quite specific, indicating that the instructions
had come from the top man, General Sherman, himself.
If they had been interpreted differently before they
reached him, he never knew it. It was Sherman's policy
to hit the enemy hard, and that his men should live off
the land. Jared had lived with it all through Georgia
and had subjected himself to much self-recrimination
during those months. The culpable men were those who
had turned him into an embittered, hardened, soulless
being who, as he stared into the green eyes of Holly
Beaufort and saw the horror and contempt she felt for
him, felt pain as though she had plunged a knife into
his heart.

It would not happen here. One place saved would
not erase what had gone before, or wipe the memory
of them from his mind, but it would be a start. A start
towards his return to a human being again, perhaps. He
considered the consequences of what he intended, and
dismissed them without further thought. In that moment
he made up his mind, and there was no going back.

Holly waited in vain for an answer. She saw that
the slate-grey eyes had darkened until they were as
stormy as the rain-clouds gathering overhead. His face
was taut, as if in pain. What terrible memories haunted
him day and night, she wondered, and knew she did
not really want to know. Haunted, yes, that was how
he looked and, suddenly, very much alone. That she
understood. The pity which came unbidden into her
heart overrode the anger she had been feeling, and
she believed his statement that Rhys had exceeded
his orders. But she did not know how to tell him this

after what had passed between them, first last night, and then now.

She saw a spot of rain fall on her sleeve, and said jerkily, 'We shall be soaked if we don't take shelter.'

He returned his attention to her as though, during those minutes of silence, he had been totally unaware of her. With a nod, he caught up the reins of both horses and indicated the trees ahead. It was only a short walk, and they managed to reach the protection of the thick oaks that grandfather Lucien had had planted, one short month after he erected the first cornerstone of the house itself, before the heavens opened over the fields. The ride home would be a worse mudbath than she had been through before, Holly mused, pulling the collar of her jacket tighter round her neck.

'Cold? Here, take a nip of this.' Jared thrust a leather-covered flask out towards her. 'Be careful, it's some of your man Joseph's corn whiskey.' Holly shook her head, but he uncapped the flask and put it to her lips. Tentatively she swallowed a small mouthful. Fire leapt down her throat and into her stomach. She gasped and coughed, watching in disbelief as Jared swallowed several large mouthfuls without turning a hair.

'How can you drink that stuff? It's fire-water!' she choked.

'Just what is needed to keep out the damp.' The flask disappeared into an inside pocket of his jacket. 'Warmer?'

'Yes. Thank you.' The last words were uttered after a pause, with hesitation, and a frown puckered his brows.

'Difficult, was it?'

'What?'

'To remember your manners?'

'I tried last night, if you remember, and look where

it got me!' She retaliated immediately, stung by his tone.
The whiskey continued its journey down into the very
depths of her stomach. It was warming, and she found
it also revived her flagging spirits. His rough handling
of her, more than the wild chase, had unnerved her,
but now her courage was returning. Her determination
not to show any weakness before this man became
uppermost in her mind once again.

'You came downstairs because I gave you no choice,'
Jared retorted. Damn the girl, why wouldn't she bend?
She looked fragile enough to snap in half in a fierce
wind, but the courage hidden within that frail shell was
immense. 'And because you had no choice, you decided
to use the situation to your advantage. Or at least to
try. I'm too old a hand to be caught at that game. It
was hard to tell you and your sister-in-law apart last
night.'

'That's unfair!' To compare her with Laurette. That
hurt more than all his anger and sarcasm!

'But true. Come now, admit it. At least let us be
honest enemies, Miss Beaufort.'

'What you say is true, only up to a point. It was my
intention to question you about the war . . . We have
had no news for so long . . .'

'You could have asked your questions at any time
since I set foot in your house,' Jared told her, a trifle
sadly. So much mistrust. He lived with it every day as
part of his life, but in this girl he found it ugly. She had
not been brought into the world for this endless struggle
to survive. She was made to be courted and loved.
Admired, cossetted, to wear fine gowns and enchant
men with her smile, not to wear herself out and grow
old before she should, assuming the responsibility of
this huge plantation and the old house she considered
a future heritage for her children and her children's

children. No, Holly Beaufort had not been brought into the world for that.

'No, Major, I could not. My pride forbade it,' Holly answered simply. 'Even as we sat at dinner, I hated myself for what I was doing. I could not bear the sight of two Union officers at the same table as myself. In the same chairs where my father and brothers have sat. It made me think of how things used to be, and then I hated you more than myself for invading my home. You have no right here, or in the South.'

'If we are going to talk about right, what right have you to hold another human being in bondage?' Jared challenged, and she coloured hotly beneath his intense scrutiny.

'I do not intend to discuss the rights or wrongs of slavery with you, Major. Suffice it to say the negroes at Tanglewood are well fed and well treated, and families are never separated. Many were born here, and consider it their home as much as I do. Joseph's wife, when she was alive, nursed me and raised me with as much love as my own mother. I miss them both terribly. If you continue on this subject, of which you have no knowledge whatsoever, I shall ride home regardless of the rain.'

'That would be very foolish. You are just recovering from one cold, do you want another?' Jared leaned back against the trunk of a tree, folding his arms. His hat was tilted back, and a damp lock of hair fell across his forehead. Holly was seized with the urge to reach out and brush it away. Clayton's hair had been unruly, too. Blond, like hers, curling about the nape of his neck. She remembered how handsome he had looked in his grey uniform, a polished sabre hanging from his side. Captain Clayton Beaufort. Deceased. Nothing could change that.

'You suddenly look very sad, Miss Beaufort. What are you thinking about?'

'One of my brothers. Clayton. We were very close.'

'I always seem to say something to make you either sad or angry.'

Holly fixed him with a suspicious look, but he met it openly.

'Why are you trying so hard to be nice, Major? It isn't like you. Honest enemies, you said. Well, then, let me tell you that I am not like Laurette. You insult me by suggesting it. Lieutenant Rhys may be welcomed in her bed, but you will not be in mine. I hope I make myself quite clear.'

'You do. You also flatter yourself,' Jared said with a contemptuous twist to his mouth. 'Whatever do you think you have to offer me?'

'The Lieutenant said you had a way about you. A charm to entice poor, unsuspecting, lonely, women to betray their husbands' trust and throw away their own honour. How many did you have in Georgia? Half a dozen? More? There will always be someone lonely enough, vulnerable enough, won't there?'

She flung the words at him, wanting to hurt him without knowing why, but he did not flinch. For an instant she saw anger flash through his eyes at the mention of the lieutenant, but it went as quickly as it had come.

'A soldier has to wear invisible armour, Miss Beaufort, in order to keep his peace of mind. If it helps you to insult me, go ahead. I have a thick hide.' Not as thick as he would have liked. Holly Beaufort had penetrated his defences, he thought to himself as she turned away and stared frozen-faced at the teeming rain. She was anxious to start back, he surmised, and to be rid of his company, not knowing that the thought could not have been further from Holly's mind.

Her words, instead of arousing him, had evoked recollections of how his arms had held her against him, his lips taken hers by storm, whether she would admit it or no. In the end, she had surrendered to the ache that had been lingering inside her since the first time they faced each other on the veranda. She was a traitor to all she had ever believed in, all she had ever said about the enemy and their ruthless ways, the behaviour of their soldiers. It was useless to deny the truth any longer. She had fought him because he had hurt her pride, but in the end she had wanted his kisses, the strength of his arms about her. Dear God, was this what loneliness did to a woman? He was right. She was as tarnished as Laurette.

Jared was watching her and frowning again as he tried to pierce her thoughts, to discover what brought such a flush to her cheeks which a moment before had been pale with cold. Her eyes met his and instantly were averted, and he knew.

Striding forward, he spun her round into his arms. His fingers clamped down over her shoulders and his face, dark and tormenting, was barely inches from hers.

'Damn you, woman, stop fighting it. You can't. Neither of us can. It's happened whether we wanted it or not. I didn't, and, by God, that's the truth.' His voice was strained, and so lacking in its usual authority, that she forgot to struggle against his hold and looked up at him, not daring to believe her ears.

'You have taken leave of your senses. Please, let me go,' Holly begged. What he was suggesting was too absurd! The truth, but not acceptable. Loneliness, that's all it was. She said so, her eyes wide, pleading silently to him to release her and to forget such words had ever been spoken between them.

He shook her and then gathered her against his chest

so hard that she felt the brass buttons of his coat pressing painfully into her breast, even through her jacket.

'No, I won't. I won't let go of what I've found. Whether it lasts for only a minute or a whole lifetime, I won't lose sight of something as wonderful as this,' Jared breathed, his lips against her hair. He had held her in his arms the night before, believing her to be a liar and a cheat like her sister-in-law, prepared to bestow favours in return for her safety and that of her home, but the minute his lips touched her, he knew he had been mistaken. In derisive anger, he had called her a child. She was. As innocent and unworldly as Laurette was cold-blooded and calculating. The soft mouth that had writhed beneath his in pain and revulsion, he suspected, had known only the kisses of brothers or the fiancé she was so loath to discuss. The body against his, tense with fear, belonged to no man. And then had come that moment of surrender, and he had had to fight against the terrible temptation which seized him, to make her belong to him, and to him alone. To show her what being a woman was all about. Sarcasm had covered the unsatisfied longing in his heart as he strode to his room, and the sound of his own whistling as he sat on the darkened balcony had helped to ease the feeling of disgust which his action had caused.

'Don't,' Holly begged. She had no defence against such words. Something wonderful—but impossible! Forbidden! 'This is wrong.'

'Perhaps, but it's happened. It's the only ray of sunlight I've had in the whole of this abominable war.'

Holly broke free of him and backed away, her features an agony of indecision. Her voice shook, but she hardly noticed, she was so distraught.

'You accuse me of being like Laurette. Now you sound like your Lieutenant. I don't believe what you say. How can I? We are enemies. There can never be anything between us except mistrust and hatred. The blood of my brothers is between us. Will always be between us.'

Jared did not attempt to touch her or go after her as she continued to back away from him. *Fool,* he thought bitterly. *Why ever did you think she would reciprocate your feelings?*

'Place any obstacles you like in our path, but they cannot demolish the fact that I was attracted to you from the first moment I saw you, and you to me. I saw it in your eyes. They gave you away, did you know that? Perhaps you didn't realise what that moment really meant?'

'Nothing,' she insisted adamantly. Then, seizing on the only possible fact she knew must deter him, she added, 'You have forgotten that I am engaged, Major. It is not fitting you should speak to me in this manner.'

'What does he look like, this captain of yours?' Jared asked softly. 'Can you remember? I thought it strange you did not mention him in the very beginning.'

'He is twenty-seven,' Holly returned sharply, 'with reddish-brown hair and . . .' she faltered, scanning her memory. She had forgotten! 'And brown eyes.'

'And you love him very much?'

She could not answer. She knew she should have lied and put an end to this farce he had begun and in which she was participating like some actress on a stage. It was unreal. She could not, and she watched those silvery eyes gleam with what she believed to be satisfaction.

'I am cold, Major Ruell. I wish to return to the house. Now.'

'Coward,' Jared mocked, but he handed her the reins of her horse and helped her into the saddle, his hands lingering longer than necessary on hers until she jerked them away.

She spurred her horse ahead of him, fearing he would try to continue the conversation, but he made no attempt to do so, or to ride beside her. Holly rode past the troopers' curious stares to the stables, slid to the ground, and tried to slip past Jared before he entered the barn, but he kneed his mount in front of her, forcing her to a halt.

'If you wish to go riding again, Miss Beaufort, please let me know.'

'I am sure I can find enough to keep me busy around the house until you and your men leave and I am free to do as I please again,' she returned stiffly. It had been so easy to drop her guard out in the open, without the milling soldiers and the orders somewhere in the background to remind her of what he was. For a few minutes they had been two ordinary people who had grown closer than was advisable under the circumstances. Had she lingered beneath the trees, listening to the softness of his voice, the spell his words had begun to weave might have entrapped her for ever. For ever? No, he was playing a game with her. He had tried a rough approach the night before, and it had failed, so he had devised a different tactic. Attracted to him? The arrogance of the man! So long as she convinced herself that he was merely amusing himself with her, that his intentions were strictly dishonourable, she was safe!

'You will not be finding the time to join us this evening, then?'

'I have no doubt Laurette is capable of keeping you both entertained.'

'Last night was one of the worst disasters of the war. Won't you allow me to make up for it? Dine with me tomorrow evening. Just the two of us, somewhere a little more private.' Jared's voice carried no further than the two of them.

'You never give up, do you, Major,' Holly snapped. 'Perhaps at your next stop there will be someone more willing to fall into your arms. Although, for her sake, I hope she thinks twice before she commits herself to such folly. No, I will not dine with you. May I go inside now?'

Wordlessly Jared turned his horse aside and she swept past him, her head held high, generations of Beaufort pride blazing from her face as she made her way to the house, looking neither left or right and oblivious to everything but the last of her dignity which she had managed to salvage intact. At a price!

'Where is he, Sergeant?' Jared demanded when Wayne met him in the hall. The man took one look at his closed face and snapped to attention. He had seen that expression before.

'If you are meaning the Lieutenant, Major, he's in the library, perusing, he says, the contents of the very interesting book collection.'

'See we are not disturbed. Did you get that old woman off to Savannah safely?'

'More or less. A bit troublesome, she was, not wanting to leave; but, as you said, Major, we couldn't let her stay on in that house with no roof and no one to take care of her. I helped her into the wagon myself and saw her on her way.'

'With compassion, I hope?' Jared grated. 'She has lost everything she had through her stupidity.'

'Major, the woman was in her sixties if she was a day. Have you ever known me to lay one disrespectful hand on an old lady?' Wayne said in a hurt tone. 'You caught up with Miss Beaufort, then?'

'Yes, Sergeant. I caught up with her.'

Tim Rhys looked up from the leather armchair in

which he sprawled, a decanter of brandy and a full glass on the table beside him. With great reluctance he climbed to his feet and came to some semblance of a rigid pose as Jared walked into the room, closed the door behind him, and just stood staring at him. No anger, no recriminations, nothing. Just that coldness of gaze that Rhys had seen many times before, especially on the battlefield.

'At ease, Lieutenant. You were standing to attention, I take it?' Jared drawled, and was pleased to see the other man look uncomfortable. Anger was no use with men of his calibre. He knew exactly how to handle his lieutenant. 'Sit down. I have something to say.'

'You managed to catch her, then? The bitch! She lied so convincingly,' Rhys began, slumping back in the huge chair. He reached for the glass at his side, gulped some of the brandy, and then, seeing Jared's raised eyebrows, said, 'Would you like a drink, Major? Good brandy, this. I've looked down in the cellars and there are another two dozen bottles. We'll take them with us when we go, eh?'

'With any luck you will drink yourself to death before we reach Columbia and save me the trouble of informing General Stanton of your behaviour these past three months. Dereliction of duty, excessive demands made on the men without my authority, not to mention the incident yesterday at the Dickinson place. If you were hoping for a promotion, Lieutenant, forget it. I'll have you stripped of your bars, and back on the march with the foot-soldiers, where you will learn a thing or two.' Jared delivered the words with the strength of a steel fist behind them. 'And while we are on the subject of misuse of your command, must I remind you that the two women beneath this roof are not like the whores you are accustomed to associating with.'

'I only know about one, first-hand.' Rhys smiled at him, and Jared barely contained his anger. It must not show, or he was lost.

'What you do with Mrs Beaufort, supposing it is with her consent . . .'

'Oh, it is. Most considerate of the needs of a poor soldier, that one.'

'If you and she wish to wallow in the gutter, then do so, but do not attempt to drag me down with you.'

'As Holly Beaufort now seems to be *your* business, we shall all be down there together, Major, shan't we? She's tarred with the same brush. Last night, didn't you find that out?' Rhys gave a loud laugh. 'Don't tell me she flashed those green eyes at you, and convinced you she was a Southern virgin saving herself for the return of her sweetheart? I wonder what she'd say if she knew her precious home was going up in flames when we leave?'

'Open your mouth to her or to anyone else—Breathe one word of our orders—And you'll hit the ground so hard you won't ever get up again! That's not a threat, Lieutenant, that's a promise, and I shall take great satisfaction in taking you apart myself before all the men, if that's what you want. I'll make you eat dirt before every single one of them.'

'That innocent face has really got to you,' Rhys began, and then the smile faded from his face. 'It's time you and I had a show-down. I want it. I'm going to have your command, Major Ruell, because you are too soft with the enemy, and you know General Sherman can't stand weakness in his men. Strength, force, batter the enemy to their knees, that's what he wants. I can do it. Your command, Major. Think on that tonight when you are looking into her eyes. Is she worth it? Because it's the price I'm going to make you pay.'

Jared selected a cigar from the humidor at his fingertips on the table. With deliberate slowness he lit it and blew a cloud of blue-grey smoke into the room.

'Only if you live, my friend. Only is you live.'

Rhys's face registered shock.

'You are a man of honour. You wouldn't dare! Is that what West Point taught you, Major?' He did not sound so confident. Had he not been drinking so much he would never have given himself away so completely, he realised, and cursed the brandy which had loosened his tongue.

'No, Lieutenant. A certain Navaho Indian called Manolito taught me that, if you are to remain totally in command, the weaker elements of your force must be eliminated. The weak and the troublesome. You think on that.'

The door closed behind him without a sound. Jaw gaping, Rhys reached for his glass. Then, with an oath which would have made even Patrick Wayne grimace, he flung it against the furthest wall.

CHAPTER
FIVE

FOR OVER an hour the next morning, Holly was closeted in the study with Joseph and Joshua, discussing the situation at Tanglewood. With the depletion of their labourers and servants, each one of them would have to do more work in the future. The spring planting demanded priority. Holly decided to send all available house servants, with the exception of Joseph and the cook, into the fields, also stable-lads and those who did menial tasks about the yards. They were going to need every hand they could get, Joshua said, and she agreed with him. If they could only keep going until the war was over and the blockade of the ports was lifted, then the cotton could be sold to give them money for badly-needed repairs.

'I shall take coffee in here,' Holly said after he had gone. She relaxed in her chair with a heavy sigh, and Joseph's gaze became concerned.

'You look tired, Miz Holly.'

'I didn't sleep very well. I'm worried, I admit it. If these soldiers had not come, we would have gone on managing quite well. Now our food supplies are dwindling, half the field hands are taking off, and we have to work doubly hard to survive. As if we didn't have enough to do in the first place. I wish they had never shown their faces here.' One face in particular. Jared's bronzed features had haunted her dreams throughout the night. His quiet voice had begged her over and over again to dine with him. She had awoke to find herself lying in bed with her hands covering her ears, so real had it all been.

'What—what do you think of Major Ruell?'

If he was surprised by her question, Joseph showed no outward sign.

'How do you mean? As a soldier or as a man?'

'Both. He puzzles me, Joseph. I find myself wanting to trust him, and I know that is wrong.' She knew she could ask the question without fear of anyone else knowing. Joseph was a close confidant and would never relate any part of a conversation between them to anyone else, not even his son.

'Considering him as a soldier, I naturally dislike the uniform he wears, but not him. I have found him straightforward in his dealings with me, and courteous, unlike that Lieutenant Rhys, who has no conception of the word gentleman. Major Ruell I consider to be a gentleman. I sense in him, I don't know quite how to describe it—a conflict of interests, perhaps. He does what he has to because he is under orders, but I am sure it weighs heavily on his mind.'

'So it should,' Holly broke in, remembering the Dickinson farm. 'Why do you think that?'

'I was outside in the hall yesterday after you returned home, Miz Holly. The Major went into the library. The Lieutenant was in there with your father's brandy. The voices were so loud I could not help overhearing what was being said. The Major was most indignant. Very cutting, he was. When he came out, his face was as black as thunder. He went past me and upstairs without even seeing me. I think he was concerned for you.'

'You credit him with a heart. I don't believe he has one.' Holly frowned at the news. Concerned for her?

That meant that everything he had said to her beneath the rain-sodden trees had been the truth! 'Go on.'

'The man I find rather a complex character,' Joseph continued, with a faint shrug. 'There are times when he has wanted to talk to me and been quite pleasant. He comes from New Orleans. His father is a lawyer. His younger brother runs the business now, with an office in Savannah. His father, being a military man, sent him to the Military Academy at West Point, and from there he was sent out west. He was just beginning to open up last night, when, for no reason, he went tighter than a clam, said good-night and pushed me out of the room. He talked like a man who doesn't find it easy to seek the company of others.'

'Maybe he was embarrassed, or annoyed at telling you so much,' Holly said. He had not told her a single fact about himself, although he professed to care for her. He had only mentioned a father and a brother. 'Has he no wife—no children?'

'No, neither. In my opinion he brought back too many memories for himself. Family, home, a past which in some way disturbs him. He was trying hard to shut out the war last night. I would like to think that for a few minutes he succeeded.'

'Thank you, Joseph. Bring my coffee, now, will you?'

When he returned with the tray of piping hot coffee and a small plate of sugared cookies, Holly turned from the window where she had been standing deep in thought for several minutes, and said, 'Will you find Major Ruell, Joseph. Ask him if he would be kind enough to dine with me tonight, about eight. I would prefer the message to be delivered when he is alone. Then ask cook to come and see me. We shall eat upstairs in my sitting-room. Prepare everything yourself.'

'Did I in some way help you to make up your mind?'
Joseph asked.

'I think you did. I wanted confirmation of what I
myself thought, I suppose,' Holly admitted. 'Don't look
at me dour-faced. We are simply going to have a quiet
meal together. I trust him. Perhaps that is foolish of
me, but I do. He will be gone soon, and we shall never
see each other again. Am I being very wrong to snatch
a few hours while I can?'

'If you were my own daughter, I would tell you to
take your happiness where you found it,' Joseph replied
gravely. 'You've had so little of it these past two years.
If his company makes you happy, then don't waste a
moment of precious time.'

'Thank you,' Holly murmured. 'I knew you would
understand and not think ill of me.'

*But should he lay a disrespectful hand on the young
mistress and betray her trust, he would never leave Tanglewood alive,* Joseph thought as he closed the door
behind him.

'Well, the Major must have made some impression on
you the other night,' Laurette declared. She came into
the bedroom that evening to find Holly being hooked
into the gown of yellow watered silk, which she knew
was the pride of her wardrobe, and as yet unworn.
Holly's hair was loose about her shoulders, but caught
up in a fine silk net of the same colour. Around her
throat she wore a magnificent creation of diamonds and
emeralds. Her grandmother's necklace. A prized family
heirloom! All this for Jared Ruell? A Yankee! 'It's
indecent that you look so ravishing. Or are you out to
steal the Lieutenant's attention as well, to compensate
him for the rough edge of the Major's tongue he received
for letting you ride off alone? He's still smarting from

whatever was said to him. He was in a foul mood last night, hardly spoke to me at all at dinner.'

'I assure you I have no interest whatever in Lieutenant Rhys. I don't care if he does not speak to me again,' Holly answered stiffly, aware of the interest growing in Mimosa's face. 'That will be all, Mimosa. I can manage alone now. I won't need you again tonight.'

Laurette's smile grew as the door closed behind the girl. She slipped down into a chair, spreading the skirts of her dress about her. She had taken extra care with her appearance tonight to win back Rhys's attention. If he saw Holly, she was lost! Her eyes were drawn to the half-open door to the sitting-room. She could just see Joseph moving about, carrying napkins and a bottle of wine. Holly was entertaining upstairs. The sly cat! At least it would keep her out of sight.

'You and the Major are not coming downstairs to-night?' she asked, her eyes considering the other girl in a most suggestive manner. For all her airs and graces, she was no better than Laurette herself. She had dismissed her maid for the rest of the evening—that meant she did not want to be disturbed. How cosy!

Holly had hoped to keep the news a secret, especially from Laurette, at least until the morning. One look at that mischievous gleam in her eyes told Holly that she suspected the worst, and would relate the news to Rhys at the first opportunity. They would misconstrue what was taking place, make loud comments and spoil what was, after all, an innocent dinner for two. No, she would not allow this evening to be spoiled by anyone. For a few hours, she too was going to shut out the war.

'No, we are dining up here.' Holly took a look at her reflection. She had lazed for over an hour in a hot bath scented with lavender. Mimosa had dried her and then rubbed sweet-smelling salve into her skin to soften and perfume it. She had prepared herself exactly as she used to do before a ball in the old days, she recollected. As though this meeting with Jared was of great importance to her. The last time she had been so fastidious had been the night of her betrothal ball, for Richard! She had thought herself to be in love then. Tonight she knew she was in love, and there was no mistake about it. When Jared had gone, what she felt would not fade. It would remain with her for ever, locked deep in her heart, unacknowledged to anyone save herself.

'You do realise the implications of such foolishness, I hope?'

Holly turned slowly and looked down at her sister-in-law with raised eyebrows. 'You, preaching to me?'

'Good heavens, no. I'm warning you to think twice about what you are about to do. What will Richard say when he finds that his devoted fiancée received a Union officer in her sitting-room, alone, and remained closeted with him all night—alone?'

'Of course you will tell him?'

'As the only other woman in the house, I feel it my duty to remind you that you, unlike I, are not free to indulge in these little . . .'

'Diversions?' Holly said cuttingly. She could hardly contain her anger. 'You may tell Richard what you wish, Laurette. It matters not to me. If you must know, I am no longer going to marry him when he comes home. That's why I went to Savannah. To see father and him. To release him.'

The colour ebbed from Laurette's cheeks. The fingers which clutched her fan showed white around the knuckles at the unexpected jolt.

'So you see, I am as free as you are,' Holly continued, noticing nothing amiss, for she was already moving towards the other room. 'Just because you have taken to the part of whore so easily, do not assume others are as eager to follow in your footsteps. The friendship which has developed between Major Ruell and myself is in no way like the sordid relationship you share with Lieutenant Rhys. I am glad Clayton is not alive to see what you have become. I think he would have killed you.'

Jared came out of his room as the grandfather clock on the landing chimed eight times. As he heard the click of the door, Sergeant Wayne quickly also stepped out into the corridor.

'I was about to knock and let you know where I shall be,' Jared said. The wily old fox must have been waiting for him! 'I am dining up here with Miss Beaufort. Why don't you relax for the evening, too?'

'A last fling before the fireworks, eh, Major?' Wayne remarked with a grin, and the smile faded from Jared's face.

'Hardly the way I would have described it, Sergeant.'

Jared strode along and knocked at the door of Holly's room, and, a moment later, entered. Wayne considered the suggestion of relaxing for the evening. That meant joining the enlisted men, who were filling their stomachs with a couple of hams they had commandeered from the smoke-house that morning, and getting drunk on the corn whiskey or brandy and wine they had tucked away in their saddlebags. It was nothing new for him. He could eat, get drunk and have a woman any time he chose, but it was not often he could just sit and enjoy the company of a friend. That was the way for him and the major, and if the latter were occupied, then he would stay in his room.

The association with Holly disturbed him. The Major was not a man for becoming deeply involved with anyone. He had always been a solitary character, preferring to keep his own counsel. Wayne liked him for that. When he did open up, he had something interesting to say, worth listening to. He had changed considerably over the years since they had first met, from a raw lieutenant, to a seasoned captain. Now a hardened campaigner, with many commendations to his name, living from day to day with no thought for tomorrow lest a bullet with his name on it destroyed plans and dreams. At least that was how it had been in 1861. Now Wayne was not so sure. In his presence only, which the sergeant considered a great honour, Jared spoke his mind, and of late he had begun to question the orders which had pushed them relentlessly through Georgia to Savannah. Just when he began to think the end was in sight, the army swung north again into South Carolina, and the orders were still the same. To destroy or commandeer property that might be profitable to the enemy. They were orders Jared Ruell had come to loathe with every breath in his body.

A last fling before the fireworks. The words hammered at Jared's brain as he stood in the sitting-room and stared at the apparition of loveliness in a yellow dress who came across and extended a ringed hand towards him. The dress seemed to float out round her like a cloud of sunlight, warming the room. Wayne's remark was pushed from his thoughts, as he took her fingers and touched them to his lips in a lingering caress that brought a flush of colour to her cheeks. She did not draw away, as he had expected, but waited for him to release her.

'What made you change your mind?'

'Joseph. He told me that you had spoken to the Lieutenant over his attitude towards me since he arrived. He said it sounded like a very personal argument. Was it, Major?' Holly asked, stepping back from him.

'There was a moment, I admit, when the urge to poke him on the jaw was almost irresistible,' Jared returned, a smile touching his lean mouth. 'We have been heading towards a confrontation for months now. If it had not been over you, something else would have brought it to a head.' He looked about him. The room had a pleasant glow from the way the candles had been placed. Beside the windows, a table was laid for two. Candles, gleaming silverware, bone china and wafer-thin glasses and, in a vase, a large bunch of bright yellow daffodils. On a side table there was a bottle of wine and one of sherry, both acquired on his passage through Atlanta. He had been keeping them for a special occasion, and could think of nothing more important than tonight. 'This is very nice. And you are looking unbelievably beautiful. If I had known this would be my reward for championing the honour of a Southern lady's good name, I might have done so sooner.'

'Are you making fun of me, Major Ruell?' Holly's eyes flashed indignantly at his light-hearted remarks. She had gone to a great deal of trouble to make him feel welcome as a way of thanking him for his concern, if that was what it was.

'I am taken aback, that's all. This is rather sudden, isn't it? Even yesterday,' and his eyes grew serious, challenging, 'when I tried to make you listen to me, you shut your ears and put your pride before you as a protective barrier to shield you from this Yankee monster who dared to speak to you of love, yet now I am received like a king in your room. This wouldn't be your way of admitting you were wrong, would it?'

He was impossible. All the trouble she had taken, and he stood before her, mocking her efforts.

'This isn't going to work,' she declared. 'You are being deliberately offensive.'

'Yes, I was,' Jared admitted. 'I'm sorry. I was putting up a barrier, I suppose, too. A final assault against an enemy far too powerful for me to overcome.'

'I don't understand what you mean.'

'What I feel for you. I tried to ignore it, and failed. I put you out of my mind, but you come into my dreams at night, my thoughts during the day. Since I got here, nothing, no one, has existed for me but you. Why don't we both stop fighting something beyond our control? Let's have a glass of wine and then sit and enjoy our meal. If you wish, only small talk. Trivialities. Anything that pleases you, but tonight neither of us is going to allow the outside world to reach us. We are immune here. Only this room exists.'

'You make it sound so easy.' Holly's lips quivered slightly. He took her hand. She thought he meant to draw her against him and kiss her, but he merely led her to the table where the wine was, filled two glasses and pressed one into her hand.

'To us, Holly Beaufort.' A teasing smile crossed his face as his eyes studied her glittering necklace. 'That looks very old and expensive?'

'My grandmother brought it with her from France when she and her husband fled to avoid the guillotine. They were aristocrats, you see. Their title was taken away from them and their lands confiscated by the new government, but they never accepted that. He, grandfather Lucien, always called himself le Duc de Beaufort. It used to infuriate him that Father would never use it.'

'He would never have approved of me here with you,' Jared said. 'He'd think I might steal your jewellery.'

'I had considered that.' Holly's eyes met his over the rim of her glass.

'How nice to know I have your complete trust.' Suddenly they were both laughing.

They sat down to cold chicken spiced with peppers, and honey-roasted ham, accompanied by salad and new potatoes. The last of those that Joshua had been able to save from the soldiers, she thought. Most of their root vegetables had been stolen within the first day. The troopers would eat well en route to Columbia. Afterwards there was apple pie with cinnamon sugar, topped with cream. Joseph brought them coffee, poured sherry for Holly and brandy for her companion, leaving the bottle within easy reach. Then he withdrew, but neither of them noticed. It had been a pleasant meal, and the hours were passing quickly. Too quickly, for Holly. She wanted to stop the clock and make time cease to exist. They had talked of families. Jared of his home and the father who was head of a now diminished family. Only Jared and his brother David were left out of the original six. The latter ran the family business because of their father's ill-health, and Jared had adhered to tradition and followed in the footsteps of his father and his grandfather and his great-grandfather and become a fighting man. A soldier.

He did not elaborate on the years which followed his graduation from military academy, and she did not press him. It was sufficient that he was confiding in her this far. She told him of her own family, her brothers and the mother, now sadly no longer with them. Of the sunny, happy days of picnicking on the lawns at Tanglewood, the barbecues and the sound of gay laughter which used to resound through the old house. She spoke of the pride of the Beauforts that had dragged them, leaving all that was dear, into a war for which they had no heart, far from home—some to die. She spoke too of the future she prayed for. The end of the war, the return of her father.

'And your fiancé?' Jared asked softly across the table, when his name was not mentioned throughout any of the conversation. 'What of him? Will you marry him when he comes home?'

She knew she should say Yes, for there was no tomorrow for them outside this room. He would leave, find himself a wife after the war and forget this brief interlude they had shared. She would never forget, but she could not tell him. She felt terribly vulnerable and afraid. In her place, Laurette would not have hesitated to grasp what was within her reach.

'Don't answer me with a lie.' Jared's eyes gleamed in the candlelight. 'I'd rather you didn't answer at all.'

'I shall not be marrying him,' Holly replied truthfully. 'Not because of—of you. I knew I had made a mistake, long ago. I was younger and foolish and I knew no better. Richard rather swept me off my feet, gave me no time to think. When I was able to consider it, I realised we had no basis for a marriage. You see, I am rather an old-fashioned girl. I shall love the man I marry.'

'Lucky man.' Jared splashed more brandy into his glass. From outside came the sound of a fiddle being played with great enthusiasm. Someone joined in with a mouth-organ. Hands began to clap in time with the music. 'My men sound as if they are enjoying themselves. They know we shall be leaving soon.' *A last fling before the fireworks!* Damn Wayne for those words. That was not why he was here with Holly!

Holly felt herself stiffen, and hoped he had not noticed. Leave! When? She dared not ask. She watched as he opened one of the french windows. The sounds of laughter reached them. The sound of enemy soldiers enjoying themselves on her food, her wine and brandy, her land; yet tonight she felt no hatred for them. Tonight the ugliness that was war did not exist for her. Only Jared Ruell existed. The candles beside him cast shadows across the handsome face. The eyes which sought hers were smoky-grey pools where wicked lights glinted an invitation, or a challenge.

'I can't remember the last time I danced with a real lady,' he drawled. 'Wait, I can. My sister, the night before I went off to this damned war. I drank too much then, rather as I am doing now, to forget what it was going to be like. I thought it was over for me, that I'd never have to use a pistol again, but fate has never dealt me a fair hand of cards. Until now. Will you dance with me outside on the balcony, Miss Beaufort?' He sketched an elaborate mock bow before her.

His words puzzled Holly. She sensed they hinted at something in his past which haunted him like a bad dream. Was that also the reason why he had drunk so much this evening? The brandy bottle was two-thirds empty, and they had both had wine with dinner. Her brief apprehension disappeared as she gazed into his face and knew she had nothing to fear. She was seized with a recklessness that overcame all caution, threw aside propriety which would never have allowed her to be seen in his company by the men below, let alone openly dancing as though, for all the world, she were enjoying herself.

Drawing aside her skirts, she returned his gesture with a graceful curtsy and rose to give him her hand. How cool his fingers were against her skin. Hers burned as if with fever. She pretended not to notice the quick glance darted her way. Jared led her out onto the darkened balcony as though he were leading her onto the dance-floor of a magnificent ballroom.

They danced without speaking. Just to be in his arms and to feel the touch of his lips on her hair, sometimes on her cheek, was enough for Holly. Two bodies merging together in the shadows, oblivious to the music from below and to the startled comment from one of the soldiers as he looked up and saw them swaying along the boardwalk, barely visible against the flower-strewn railings and dim walls—except for the yellow material of Holly's dress, which from time to time was caught in the flickering firelight.

The fiddle music ended, and then began again, this time with a waltz.

'They don't exist,' Jared murmured as she stopped, realising that they had been seen. Her cheek returned to rest against his jacket and they continued to dance. Nothing mattered. Not them, not Laurette, not Richard. Only Jared and herself!

The inevitable happened. It had to. Her face was too close to his, those soft lips, slightly parted, were too inviting. Her eyes were closed, her face so serene and content. He would remember it for the rest of his days. It was all he would have. One more thing he would take with him. The memory of what might have been.

Her body curved into his as he guided her back into a darkened doorway. Her arms stole up to fasten around his neck as his mouth sought hers. Not as before, hurriedly, brutally, in a determined effort to overcome all resistance. But slowly, almost hesitantly. Imprisoning them, cherishing them, until he realised how eagerly they answered his. As quickly as the esctatic moment had come upon them, it was broken, as Holly pulled herself from his embrace and ran back into the sitting-room, with something that sounded suspiciously like a sob.

Jared followed slowly, taking his time, forcing down

the anger which had risen in him. She had no comprehension of the depth of his feelings. How those few moments had roused him to a possessive madness he had never known before with any woman. It was not her fault. He loved her for her unworldly innocence.

'You are thinking about what Rhys told you.' It was framed as a statement, rather than a question, and she did not answer, but stood looking at him, her eyes full of misery. Those nameless, faceless women he had known during the past four years had risen unbidden in her mind even as she was enjoying his kisses, to taunt her and create suspicion. 'I've never denied there were others. Why should I? I have no wife, no sweetheart. No commitments of any kind.'

'Did that give you the right to misuse them?' The words were uttered before she could snatch them back. Jared's eyes narrowed to angry slits. His mouth went taut as if she had struck him.

'Good God, girl! I've never taken any woman like that. Is that what you believe of me? Why haven't I taken you, then, if that's all I want? I've had enough opportunities.' The harshness of his voice made her wince. He spoke the truth. The other night outside her room. Yesterday in the rain. Tonight . . . 'On the rare occasions it happened, and they were not frequent—I have neither Rhys's over-inflated ego nor his capacity for enjoying the discomfort of my fellow human beings —they were bored wives, sick to death of being alone, no one to shower them with compliments, escort them to picnics and balls. Weary of having to soil their lily-white hands and work for a change. They would have bedded with any man who half smiled at them. For all I know, they've done it before. I'm certain they will do it again. Half of them were part-whore inside, like Laurette. Do I shock you? Why? Women get as lonely as men, you know. Only not all of them give such willing aid and comfort to the enemy! You still think that's what I want from you, but you are wrong. What I want, you can't—won't—give me,' Jared ended stonily.

'What—what is that?' Holly trembled beneath his gaze. She knew every word was true and hated herself for the pain she had caused him. The trust she had probably destroyed.

'Your love. Out there a minute ago, when I held you, you wanted me as much as I did you. I felt it. Is that why you ran in, because you were afraid of yourself?'

He saw bright tears start to her eyes and then slide slowly down cheeks blenched of all colour, and knew he had guessed right.

'Holly. Oh, Holly, don't.' He held her tightly and kissed them away. 'I didn't mean to hurt you. I was angry.'

'I—I cried when Robert died. I promised myself I would not cry again. I would be strong enough to withstand any shock, any hardship. I would not be a weak, tearful woman. You said I acted like a man, do you remember?'

'I was a fool, and a blind one to boot,' Jared said in a fierce whisper. 'You are all woman. Beautiful, desirable—unattainable.'

She drew back, but did not move outside the circle of his arms. Her fingers strayed to the necklace at her throat. Slowly she unfastened the catch, slid it into one hand and offered it to him.

'Take this when you go. With it goes my love and the knowledge I shall be here—if you want to return when the war is over. Perhaps, if you look at it enough in the months to come, you might think the prospect worth coming back to.'

The shock of her words jarred him. For a long while

he did not move, or attempt to take the necklace. With a smile, Holly placed it inside his jacket, against his heart.

'Carry me with you, Jared, wherever you go,' she pleaded, and then her voice broke and she buried her face against the hard material, afraid of seeing rejection on his face.

Gently he turned it up to his, and she almost wept again at the sight of the passion blazing from his eyes. Again Jared found himself on the edge of that chasm, teetering precariously, yet still able to regain some of his balance.

'You may not want me to come back.' He almost blurted out the truth. He silently cursed Sherman, Rhys, the war, himself, knowing none of it did any good. He was beyond help. 'In time, you may think of me in the same light as Richard. Would you really be proud to walk beside me, Holly, in front of your father, relatives, friends, knowing where I have been, what I have done? I was at Atlanta. So was your brother Clayton. Have you thought about that?'

'Yes. I thought about it very carefully, but it makes no difference to the fact I am in love with you. Nothing can change that,' Holly said in a small, but proud, tone. 'Nothing, do you hear?'

Jared put her away from him, visibly moved. He would come back. Somehow he would make it possible. How did he find a miracle?

'Tonight you would not be safe with me,' he said quietly. 'And I don't want that on my conscience when I leave. Contrary to what you may believe, I do have one. Go to bed, Holly.'

'Stay—if you need proof of my love.'

'I carry the proof with me.' Jared knew she had never uttered such an invitation in her life before. A terrible hunger seized him. The future he had never possessed, the myth that haunted him when it was so readily available to those around him, had suddenly become reality for him, too. He would not destroy it. He kissed her once more, tenderly, but without emotion. The moment of danger had passed for them both. 'I love you. Remember that. Trust me! Good-night.'

'Good-night.' Holly clung to him, but again he gently eased her away and pushed her towards the door of her bedroom. Stood waiting until it closed behind her and he was alone. Waited for the sound of the key being turned in the lock, but heard nothing. She trusted him that much!

'Everything all right, sir?' Wayne just happened to appear as Jared strode past his door. Still fully dressed at half-past midnight, and not a smell of drink on his breath. Jared was amazed.

'We leave in the morning. Sun up.'

'I'll organise the men.'

'No. I'm giving Lieutenant Rhys that pleasure,' Jared said, his lips broadening into a smile. 'Now.'

Without announcing himself, he flung open the door of Rhys's room and strode in. From the direction of the bed, Laurette gave a squeal of horror and shot beneath the covers. The lieutenant started to rise, then, remembering his state of undress, fell back into the bed.

'Make the men ready to move out first thing, Lieutenant,' Jared ordered, without blinking an eyelid.

'Now?' Rhys's face deepened into an ugly frown as he realised what was behind the order. Wayne had warned him not to cross Jared Ruell, but he had been too stubborn to listen. He'd see him in hell for this interruption.

'Now, Lieutenant.'

'Just because she's turned you down, you don't have

to take it out on those of us who have had better luck,'
Rhys flung after him as Jared turned back to the door,
and he froze, his jaw tightening.

Struggling into his clothes, the man came after him.
Jared turned and hit him just once. The blow sent him
sprawling to the floor at the foot of the bed. Laurette's
face appeared, saw the murderous look on Jared's face,
and disappeared again with a muffled scream.

'You hit me.' Rhys rubbed his chin; stunned, then
angry, then grinning with satisfaction. Repeating, 'You
hit me. Did you see that, Sergeant? He hit me, without
provocation. Deliberately.'

From the doorway Patrick Wayne regarded him with
an air of puzzlement.

'Hit you, Lieutenant? I'm sorry, sir. From where I'm
standing, it looked as if you tripped over your trousers.'

Jared slammed the door behind them and headed
back towards his own room. Wayne followed, waiting
for orders.

'Thank you, Sergeant. I owe you,' Jared said at
length. Rhys's threats did not bother him. He forgot
them as he touched the object in his pocket. Wayne's
eyes followed his hand and wondered what he carried.
Maybe, in time, he would know.

'No, sir. Not you. Besides, I've been wanting to do
the same thing ever since the little Welsh rat joined us.
You go back to the lady, Major, and I'll make sure you
are not disturbed for the rest of the night.'

'The lady has retired and I won't be joining her.'
Jared went into his room and motioned the man to
follow. 'Come in and have a drink if you can spare the
time.'

'Thanks, Major. I thought you'd never ask.'

An hour later, when Wayne had weaved his way from
the room, having consumed the best part of a bottle of

Joseph's corn whiskey to which he had become willingly addicted, Jared stood by the window, listening to the muted sounds of activity below. He had sent Wayne to oversee the departure preparations without Rhys being aware of it, but despite that precaution, he knew it would not prevent what would happen. Orders were orders. But, this time, only up to a point. Even that would not stop Holly from hating him in the morning. Tossing his jacket across a chair, he loosened his collar and felt the cold night air on his skin like an icy hand of doom. In the morning he would be leaving Tanglewood and the girl he loved. What they had shared this evening might well have been obliterated by what he had to do beforehand. *Trust me,* he had asked her. In her place, he knew he would find it impossible. Turning away, he reached for the bottle and drained it into a glass. For a few short hours, at least, he could shut out tomorrow and the knowledge of what he must do to her and the hardship and suffering his actions would cause. *God forgive me,* he thought bitterly as the whiskey slid down his throat, burning like hell-fire. She never would!

CHAPTER
SIX

THE SOUND of someone screaming awoke Holly with a start. For an instant she thought she was dreaming again, reliving that awful moment when Mimosa had come flying up to the house, four days ago now, to tell her the Yankees were coming. It was no dream. It went on and on. Not Mimosa, then who? Laurette! She leapt from the bed, pulling on a robe as she ran to the door.

Laurette stood in the corridor in her nightclothes, tears streaming down her cheeks. Holly realised at once that she was hysterical, and hesitated for a moment only before slapping her soundly.

'Be quiet! Calm yourself,' she said, gripping her firmly by the shoulders. From below she could hear the sound of voices and of breaking glass. An icy hand clutched at her heart. Troopers in the house? Where was Jared? 'What's happening? For goodness sake, control yourself and tell me.'

'He took everything while I was asleep,' Laurette sobbed. She pushed back the hair shadowing her face, and Holly was shocked to see that the tears were of rage, not fear. Her eyes burned as she stared at the other girl. 'He ransacked my room.'

'Who did?'

'That damned Lieutenant! He has stolen my jewellery and all my money. He's leaving . . . Your precious Major has turned them loose on the place.' She laughed harshly at the horror registering on Holly's face. 'You hear me? They tricked us. The soldiers are going to leave us with nothing. They meant it to be like this from the beginning.'

A stream of unladylike abuse poured from her lips that at any other time would have made Holly cover her ears with her hands, but now she was too shocked to care that Laurette not only acted like a guttersnipe, but swore like one, too, when the fancy took her.

She took to her heels and ran to the head of the stairs. Blue-coated men were moving from room to room. She saw pictures torn from their frames lying on the carpet, ornaments disappearing into sacks held by eager soldiers who were, some of them, little more than boys. The library door gaped open. The floor was littered with her father's precious books, many first editions. Covers had been ripped away in a mad hunt for money and valuables. Forcing down a sob of panic, she turned and rushed wordlessly past Laurette and into her bedroom, slamming the door behind her. She took all but a few trinkets from her jewel-case, thrust them into the velvet pouch which lay at the bottom of the box, and looked desperately around for a hiding-place. If the troopers came upstairs, they would tear the place apart. Nowhere would be safe for the fortune of precious stones she held.

In feverish haste, she flung off the robe, dressed, and pushed the pouch deep into the bosom of her shift. Fastening the buttons of the dress high about her neck, she went downstairs. She was not going to let the Yankees leave without a fight. In the pocket of her skirts nestled the Derringer Jared had returned to her. One shot only. For him. For the betrayer of her trust! Her love! *'Your precious Major has turned them loose on the place,'* Laurette has said. She could not believe it! Yet, if it were not true, why were there soldiers everywhere, destroying what they could not carry. Ransacking cupboards, running from the house with armfuls of booty. She felt sick to see it, and her steps flagged, but doggedly she pushed herself on downstairs. She came face to face with Lieutenant Tim Rhys.

He was loading silver and cut glass into the sack held for him by an orderly. She caught at his arm, screaming at him to stop, but he flung her aside with a fierce blow that made her senses reel.

'Stay clear of me, woman, or I'll put a torch to this place anyway.'

'Burn—burn the house?' The ultimate horror. 'No! You wouldn't!'

'Yes, he would, and would sit on his horse and watch it burn, laughing.' Laurette spoke dully from the chair where she had been unceremoniously tossed some while before after the lieutenant had knocked her unconscious as she tried to scratch out his eyes with her long nails. A vivid bruise was already beginning to show on the pallor of one cheek. She looked dejected, cowed, Holly thought, yet her tongue had the sting of a viper as she went on, 'Don't made him mad, Holly. The Lieutenant has a penchant for hitting women and old men. He knocked out Joseph when he came to help me,' she added by way of explanation. 'He and Mimosa are under guard with the other servants in the kitchen. The men looked at her like dogs on heat. It was disgusting. As if they haven't had enough women these last few days.'

'Oh, dear God, no!' Holly said weakly. She felt a wave of nausea sweep over her and clutched at a chair for support. 'This—this isn't with the knowledge of Major Ruell. It can't be!'

Rhys laughed in her face and gained immense satisfaction from the knowledge that he was in a position to destroy them both.

'This has been happening all the way through Georgia, little lady—under his command. The Major is a soldier through and through; sticks to his orders, no matter what. I thought he was going to welch on this place, but it doesn't look that way any more. That's it, Private. Get this stuff out of here and call the other men. They've had time enough for what they wanted.'

'You animal,' Holly hissed, her fists clenching. For a moment she considered using the valuable bullet in the Derringer on him. No, he was not worth it.

'Animal. That reminds me,' Rhys grinned, stuffing a small jade Buddha into his pocket—Holly had bought it for her father's last birthday before the war. 'The Major has an eye for good horseflesh as well. At this moment he's in your stables helping himself to the best he can find.'

Holly ran from the room, with the sound of his mocking laughter following her down the steps and across the open space which led to the stables and paddocks. She brushed aside hands that reached out to restrain her, shut her ears to the coarse remarks and invitations which followed in her wake. She did not think of it until afterwards, but no one seriously attempted to detain her.

Sergeant Wayne, whom she had passed without seeing, stepped into the room she had vacated and came to attention before Rhys, his face impassive.

'Begging the Lieutenant's pardon, but the Major gave strict orders the house was not to be touched.'

'I'm not touching the house, damn you! I'm having it stripped.'

Wayne's hand fell to his holster. Deliberately he snapped it open and waited.

'The Major expects the men to be rolling out of here

in five minutes, sir. I'm to stay here and make sure the place is empty. Save for the women, that is.'

'You ignorant Irish peasant,' Rhys snapped. 'Draw that weapon and I'll break you with him.'

'That might be a little difficult, Lieutenant, if you were dead,' Wayne returned, and there was a hint of a smile on the craggy features. 'As this is between the two of us, I'd welcome the chance to blow your head off. Sure now, I'm begging you to give me the opportunity before anyone comes in to find us.'

A sheet of flame shot up from the building in front of the stables. Holly came to an abrupt halt. The hope that Jared somehow knew nothing about all this died inside her as, ashen-faced, she watched three years of cotton go up in flames. Three years' work and money. Without that, Tanglewood would never get back on its feet again. The Confederate money in the bank in Savannah was all but useless and bought very little. A family of hogs dashed across her path, squealing in terror. Behind them came four soldiers, laughing at each other's attempts to catch the elusive creatures. She was not amused by the sight. What, if anything, would be left when the soldiers had gone? Wagons were being loaded with sacks of grain, badly-needed grain for the spring planting. Trussed chickens and turkeys followed, armfuls of vegetables with the wet soil still clinging to their roots.

Everything, Holly thought in despair. They were taking everything. Smoke choked her as she ran to the stables. She stood in the doorway, wiping her streaming eyes with the back of her hand. That same terrible coldness settled over Jared as he turned and saw her, and realised that the moment of reckoning had come. There was nothing he could say to soften the blow, yet he tried, because he loved her and wanted to come back to this tranquil haven where he had found peace and contentment and a woman with whom he wanted to share the rest of his life.

Outraged, Holly stared past him to the horses being roped together by another soldier. They were the best of her stables, among them her own mare.

'You are even lower than the men you command,' she screamed. 'The men you are allowing to pillage and rape and destroy. You are taking my horses! How can we do the spring ploughing without them?'

She spoke of horses, not of what had passed between them, Jared thought startled. Rape? What did she mean? His orders had been explicit.

'Who?' He stepped towards her, eyes narrowing.

'Don't come near me! The Lieutenant left men to watch Mimosa and the other women. He hit Joseph when he went to help Laurette. How brave you Yankees are! You make war on women, too. How proud you must be of yourselves. You are taking our food, do you know that?'

'I have my orders. Holly, listen to me . . . I tried to tell you last night, but I couldn't. I couldn't spoil something so wonderful—and it was. Don't let it die because of this. I'm leaving you enough food to see you through until spring, and there are horses back in the stalls for your ploughing. I should take everything, but I'm not going to. I can't. You know why.'

'No, Major Ruell, I don't,' Holly said in such a cold tone that he wondered whether she had gone into shock at what she had seen. Her eyes had a blank look in them, even as they stared right at him. Large green pools of emptiness. 'Why not take it all? Why didn't you last night? Then you would have completed a most successful mission, wouldn't you? You and Rhys could have compared notes on the way to Columbia.' Her words slammed into him with the force of a cannon-shell. The hand he held out was ignored.

'Holly,' he said softly. 'For the love of God, listen to me. Don't send me away like this. I'm begging you to listen.'

'You don't have to be nice to me any more, Major. There's no need to make things easy for yourself, now you are leaving.'

'Easy!' Jared swore aloud. 'Do you think this is easy for me? I'm under orders, you little fool! I'm ignoring part of them, as it is, to help you.'

'For a man who has been doing the same thing all the way through Georgia and, for all I know, ever since the war began, I should say it is very easy for you.' Holly spoke as if she had not heard him. 'You have had so much practice. If you had taken me last night, I think I could not hate you more than I do now.'

'You are overwrought,' Jared said, restraining the urge to touch her. Shock. Yes, that was it. It would pass, and when she thought about it, she would realise he had had no choice in the matter. The house had been spared. He had been able to do that for her at least. So little, but a roof over her head was better than the shelter of trees or nothing at all, which is how he had left some wretched families. Whatever happened when he reached Columbia, and the final showdown came between himself and Lieutenant Rhys, he would know she was safe, with Joseph and Joshua to care for her until her father returned. If he did not, she would manage. She had the heart of a lion, and a bite to match when need be. He could do no more.

'The men are moving out, Major,' Sergeant Wayne said from the doorway. Jared nodded tersely, his eyes still intent on Holly's agonised features. The pain there!

'It was no lie last night. Any of it,' he said in a low

tone, stepping close to her. Before he rode out of her life, he had to make her believe it. It was all he had left from the carnage he had been forced to create.

Holly lifted her eyes to his. Would they ever shine again, he wondered? The eyes of the living dead. Of people breathing the air, but not a part of the world about them. And then they were suddenly lucid, and he felt a pang of fear strike him. A different kind of fear from anything he had known before during his years as a soldier.

'Oh, that!' A small bubble of laughter rose in her throat. 'You did not think I was serious, did you, Major? Two can play at that game.'

A mist swirled before Jared. The lovely face contorted with derision mocked him beyond all reason. Reacting, without thinking, his palm came up and dealt her a stinging blow across the face. No tears came—the smile remained. The eyes now smouldered with hate. It was what she had hoped he would do. The pain had brought her to her senses before she weakened and begged him to tell her he loved her still, that he would come back to her despite the havoc he had wrought here today, the hardship it was going to cause in the months ahead. Had he touched her as last night, with gentleness, she knew she would have responded and started along a path of humiliation and degradation from which there would be no turning back. She drew a deep breath and tossed back her head. Proud, once more, in control of herself. She was Holly Beaufort, mistress of Tanglewood, and he was the enemy. It was over!

'One day you will have cause to remember those words. I'm coming back when this war is over and I'm going to make you eat crow for what I'm feeling. I'm going to humble that Southern pride and you'll beg my forgiveness. Do you hear? I'll see you on your knees,'

Jared said in clipped tones. Lies! All of it lies! What an actress! And he had begged her to trust him!

As he swung himself into the saddle, Holly's fingers closed round the Derringer in her pocket. Jared's eyes caught the furtive movement. He knew immediately what she had hidden there. His smile was ugly as he nudged his horse close to her.

'From this distance, you shouldn't be able to miss, Holly. I'll be dead, but you will be, too. Wayne will see to that, and then what will happen to this place? That's all you really care about, isn't it? What last night was all about? Good heavens, Laurette could take lessons from you. You were good . . . I actually believed the lies that came from that treacherous little mouth. I must have been too long in the field. Remember what I said. I'm coming back. Best save that bullet for then. Be proud of yourself. I believed you.'

Wayne's hand was resting on the butt of his pistol, Holly saw. Slowly she withdrew her own from her pocket. Jared thought at first it was relief he felt, then realised it was disgust. For her, himself, the whole messy war and the poor fools who were caught helplessly up in it.

'Perhaps you won't come back, Major Ruell.' Her voice had all the velvety softness of a ripe peach containing a deadly poison. His hand tightened over the reins, steeling himself for what was to come, but even so he was not prepared for the terrible words which dropped from her lips. 'Why should a man like you live when good men like my brothers have died? May God in his infinite mercy guide the aim of some Confederate soldier somewhere along the way. I hope you die, too, do you hear me? I shall pray for it every night until this war is over . . .'

'Holly! No!' Jared cried. 'You can't mean it.' She

did! There was no retraction, no softening of the hard expression on the lovely face upturned to his. She wanted him dead! He sent his horse careering out of the barn at such a reckless pace that she had to jump back to avoid being trampled down.

Sergeant Wayne stared down at her where she lay, her eyes widening at the realisation of what she had done. She had sent the man she loved into battle with her death-curse hanging over his head. No! No! She was not aware she cried out in her horror and grief. She faintly heard the man in front of her threaten, 'If he doesn't come back to settle with you, I will.' And then he, too, was gone and she was alone. Alone with the memory of what she had done.

Behind the column of soldiers, black smoke billowed into the air. Jared did not look back as he joined them. He had seen it before and it gave him no pleasure. This time especially.

Rhys slowed his mount to come level with him, stared curiously into the closed face, and wondered what had taken place to put him in such a bad mood. He knew that look, the narrowed eyes, dark like smouldering embers, but still he asked, 'What about the house? We could still put the torches in. Strip it first, of course. It was a veritable goldmine, Major. Neither of us need leave empty-handed.' Not that he was. Two bulging sacks hung from his pommel. A loaded horse was being looked after by an orderly whom he could trust—to a certain extent.

'Get up front, Lieutenant. Send two men a mile ahead to scout. Report to me when they return, and not before.' Jared could barely be bothered to speak to him. It was the end for him, he realised, but he did not care. He would not fight to keep his command if Rhys challenged him in front of his superiors. Let him be the proud leader of a bunch of ruthless, thieving, butchers. They had not started out that way. Once they had been normal men, but that's what they were now, and he had had enough of it.

Scowling, the lieutenant thought it wiser to obey than question further. At a bend in the drive, Jared stopped and looked back at the house, partly obscured by smoke and flames from the outlying buildings. With luck they would bring it under control before the wind increased. Negroes were running up and down about the place, carrying buckets, trying to save furniture, personal effects, foodstuffs. Unconsciously his fingers stole to the hard object over his heart.

'*I'll be back,*' he had said to a girl who could not hear him, did not want to hear him, but would remember his words, and wonder and wait.

'Did you say something, Major?' Wayne enquired, looking back over his shoulder.

'Yes, Sergeant. Move out at the double!'

April brought with it a wealth of colour in the gardens outside the house, and the lawn began slowly to return to the beautiful lush grass that Holly thought had been damaged beyond repair by the horses of the Yankee soldiers. The heavy scent of roses filled the air. She walked along the pathways, filling her nostrils with it and that of honeysuckle and lilac, feeling for the first time the warmth of the sun on her bare shoulders. The weather had been improving for the past month, but she had noticed neither the brilliant sunshine nor the new vegetables pushing their way through the red-brown earth to announce that months of hard work had not been in vain. She did not see the mended paddock fences, or the half-finished barn Joshua himself was undertaking to repair in what little spare time he had. Nothing had mattered. Nothing had been important enough to rouse her from the world of shadows in which she had lived since the day Jared Ruell had ridden out of her life.

She walked, ate, slept. She rode beside the huge negro, who watched her in silence and offered no words of comfort to ease her suffering, as Joseph and Mimosa tried to do and somehow managed to keep the plantation going. She worked alongside the hands who remained, sowing new cotton-seeds, vegetables for the house. Her foresight had saved them, but for a few months only. The grain hidden away, the seeds she had hoped would help them to survive for at least a year, all were now gone.

One barn still had its roof, apart from the one under reconstruction. The stables had been badly burned when red-hot cinders had blown into the eaves. By the time a bucket-chain had been formed, the roof had gone, and she had lost one of the ploughing horses. The nightmare of that day never left her. She moved about the place like some mechanical doll, responding to Laurette's questions, even Joseph's gently-spoken words of encouragement for her brave efforts, with anger. It was all she had left. A deep, burning anger for all she had lost. Anger and love jostled and tumbled inside her until she thought she would go mad trying to disentangle them.

And then, this bright morning, as she sat on the porch waiting for Joseph to bring her coffee before she rode out again with Joshua to sow the last of the corn-seed along the river bank, she was aware of a peace she had not known for months settling over her like a soothing hand upon a feverish brow. Jared was gone. He would never come back, despite his threat. She had to pick up the threads of her life, to put together what he had sought to tear apart. What she had almost allowed him, in her foolishness, to destroy. Tanglewood is all you care about, he had said. He was right. For her, nothing else mattered now. The rebuilding of the wrecked buildings, the next crop of cotton, the welfare of herself and Laurette and the negroes. That was important to her. Nothing else. When her father returned home, he would be proud of her and he would never know how close she had come to betraying the trust he had placed in her. One day, when she had enough courage, she would tell him of the man who stole her love, defiled it, threw it back in her face. Love! She never wanted to know such bitter-sweet agony again. She was done with it for ever.

If she and Joshua had not taken the steamboat to Savannah to try to buy grain, she would never had discovered that the war was over. At least not for weeks, perhaps months, until remnants of the Confederate army began to drift back to their homes. For the first time in a year, she saw papers and read of the disintegration of the Southern army, the surrender of General Lee at Appomatox on the ninth of April, and that of his brave soldiers in the days immediately following. The war was all but over. There was a paragraph in the latest edition, itself four days old, with the news, speculating that General Johnston and the last remaining Confederate forces had been offered surrender terms by General Sherman. How she hated that man. His name made her think of the orders which had brought Jared Ruell to Tanglewood. The orders which had destroyed her life, her peace of mind.

She spent a whole afternoon reading. Fayetteville in North Carolina had been taken by General Slocum and the 14th Corps of Federal troops on the tenth of March. Sherman marched triumphantly into the city the following day. She could not help wondering whether Major Jared Ruell had been among the victorious forces. Gradually the list grew longer. Minor skirmishes, battles in small towns and valleys with strange-sounding names, all leading to the same thing. The defeat of the South and its ultimate surrender to the North. Columbia was overrun, and for a while had the dubious honour of entertaining the whole Union army under Sherman. The fire which had been started by the retreating cavalry of Major Wade Hampton—her heart leapt, for this was her father's commanding officer and she knew where at least he was now—had been fanned by a fierce breeze and gone out of control. With a little help from the enemy, it was hinted, it had spread and destroyed the heart of Columbia before being curbed.

When Holly and Joshua returned to Tanglewood, they brought with them only a quarter of the grain she had set out to buy, and that had been purchased at ten times the normal cost. She had sold two pieces of jewellery to cover the exorbitant price, only receiving half of what they were worth, but she did not care. Tanglewood still continued to function, despite its depleted workforce, Laurette's constant complaining and lack of enthusiasm for the chores forced upon her and despite the dismal prophecy of the bank manager in Savannah who had advised the sale of Tanglewood as soon as possible. The money from its sale would cover the loan Holly's father had obtained at the outbreak of war. He had borrowed to provide badly-needed uniforms, horses and guns for the local plantation-owners and men willing to enlist, she realised. Fearing that the war might be prolonged, he had not wanted to touch their savings. Now that money was in the bank vaults—useless! And she still owed. It was a setback she had not anticipated.

On her return, Laurette met her with a letter. Holly opened it in silence. It was written by a nun of the Sisters of Charity in Goldsboro informing her that Colonel John Beaufort had been wounded at a place called Bentonville and brought to them for care. Wounded, but alive!

Slowly grey-uniformed figures, tattered, often on foot, limping, being carried, or slouching dull-eyed along the dusty roads, husbands, sons and sweethearts began the tortuous journey homewards. Many found their houses destroyed, families dead or moved to places of safety with relatives or friends. Many dropped and died by the wayside, in ditches and fields, through sheer exhaustion, starvation, or the lack of will to survive in a conquered land. The spirit that had kept them going for so long was broken, Holly realised as she watched them pass through Tanglewood over the following weeks. Compassion, stronger than her own needs, made her feed them whenever possible, offer shelter, however primitive. It tore her heart apart to see them so dejected and beaten, but strengthened her fierce determination to remain unconquered and to survive.

May came and went without any more news from Goldsboro about her father's progress, so in desperation she wrote to the Sisters of Charity asking if she could come and fetch him as soon as he was able to travel. Just to have him near at hand would instil fresh courage into her, she knew. The orange crop was doing well, but many of the lemon-trees, badly mutilated by the soldiers with deliberate malice before they left, failed even to show blossom. Next year, she prayed, grateful that they had some fruit at least. She spent a whole day with cook making jam, working just as hard as if she was out in the fields or sewing curtains and cushion-covers for the house, or mending sheets that would have been discarded before the war. There was nothing with which to replace them now, and there would not be until their financial situation improved.

That evening for tea there was hot bread straight from the oven, spread thickly with the newly-made jam. As she watched everyone tucking into it with real enthusiasm, Holly felt very happy. Such a small thing, to bring such great satisfaction. Only Laurette ate sparingly, complaining that the hefty wedges of fresh bread would thicken her waistline. She always complained at mealtimes, reminding them all so unnecessarily of the meals served at Tanglewood in the past. Succulent duck, roasted in wine and served with masses of gravy. Ham and chicken cooked a hundred different ways. Chocolate cookies and sugared biscuits, strawberry cakes oozing with cream.

Holly knew it was no use to chide her for her thoughtlessness. It was her way, and she would never change. Each day she grew more discontented with the way of life around her, the poverty and the boring meals. The fact that she had not only to work alongside Mimosa and cook at odd times in the kitchen, but to sit at the same table with them to eat. Holly had found the work of the house servants to be considerably lessened if everyone ate in the kitchen in the evening and enjoyed one wholesome meal. Most of the day she was too busy to break off for lunch and nibbled at small cakes or biscuits, if their meagre rations allowed the baking of such items, and they did not take up too much time from the jobs in hand.

She had lost weight over the months. The high cheek-bones stood out now with more prominence, making her eyes look even larger. The soft hands, that had been petted and kissed by handsome young men as they danced with her, were often red and calloused from manual labour. She wore her hair in a long thick plait down her back. She did not want to cut it, even though it was becoming exceedingly unmanageable, and this was the best way she had found to keep it away from her face when she was working. She would have to do something with her appearance before she went to fetch her father, she thought, one day as she stared at herself in the mirror. She looked like the hard-working wife of a penniless 'cracker', which was the name Southerners gave to homesteaders or farmers with smallholdings, instead of the mistress of a vast plantation. She would have to find a suitable gown, too. She could not present herself before him like a pauper. She ought to cut up and alter the yellow watered silk, which she had pushed to the back of the closet the day after Jared had ridden away. She had no use for it as it was.

On the morning that she and Mimosa spread the dress out on the sitting-room floor, and sat on each side of it discussing whether it could be altered, a rebel soldier rode up the drive to the house and was admitted by Joseph.

Attracted by Laurette's excited squeals of delight, Holly hurried downstairs. She did not at first recognise the gaunt, heavily bearded, soldier. The last time she had seen him he had been astride a chestnut stallion belonging to Clayton, resplendent in grey broadcloth trimmed with gold. A negro body-servant had held the reins of his horse as he bent down to kiss his cousin good-bye. Richard Mitchell, Holly's fiancé, had returned to Tanglewood, and with him he brought the news of the death of Colonel John Beaufort. He had died three days after Holly had received the letter from the Sisters of Charity. That day, although no one ever knew it, another part of her also died.

Holly was beside herself with anger as she waited on the veranda for Richard to return to the house. He had taken Laurette riding, for the third time that week. The rest of his time he divided between the duties of an overseer, which he had taken upon himself without prior consultation with Holly, or her approval now that he had done so. One morning he had calmly told Joshua to return to the fields with the rest of the hands, and had himself assumed the negro's work. She had not discovered this until nearly a week later. She had thought he was merely being helpful, realising the huge task she had taken upon herself. How dare he presume without one word to her! And to treat Joshua so ungraciously! Had it not been for him and the powerful sway he held over the remaining negroes at Tanglewood, she would have had no labour at all.

Richard had changed since she had last seen him. This she had expected, but there was also a difference in his manner towards her which she found disturbing. An intimacy which went beyond the bounds of propriety she still clung to doggedly in his presence, as if it would wipe out—as if anything could—that night with Jared and the recklessness of mood which had driven her uncaring into his arms, declaring her love. He never missed an opportunity to touch her, to try to kiss her. His kisses seared her lips, frightening her. They demanded so much more than she was willing to give, as once before. She shuddered to think of the women with whom he had gained such experience.

Several times she had attempted to tell him that she considered their engagement no longer binding, but as if sensing what she was about to say and unwilling to accept his release, Richard began to talk of the war. The horrors of the men he had seen killed, the motherless children wandering about Atlanta as fire raged through the city. The hunger and deprivations he had suffered as the army continued to retreat. How he had managed to arrive at Tanglewood on horseback only because the soldier who owned the mount had fallen dead by the roadside in front of him.

Each time her sympathy was aroused, Holly remained silent, reproving herself for not allowing him a little more time to relax in more comfortable surroundings than he had known for the past four years, to eat when the fancy took him, to ride aimlessly about the plantation, knowing that no bluecoats would appear to chase him, to sleep in a soft bed at night, warm and safe. She was being selfish and must not rush things. She had already told him he was welcome to stay with them as long as he pleased. The right time would come soon, she told herself.

But as the weeks slipped by, Richard seemed to have no inclination to leave Tanglewood, and more and more assumed the role of master of the house. On several occasions Holly had cause to speak to him for reprimanding Joseph without her knowledge, or for countermanding her orders about something relating to the everyday running of the plantation.

To discover that he had usurped Joshua and now considered himself to be running the plantation was the straw that broke the camel's back.

By the time Richard and Laurette returned from their morning ride, she had decided she must tell Richard of her change of feelings towards him. That, if anything, would encourage him to think about leaving. Laurette positively glowed in his company, she thought, as she watched him help her sister-in-law to the ground and she inwardly grimaced at the warm smile directed at him. Comfort and solace to the enemy, now to homeless soldiers back from the war. Was she being ungracious in her thoughts? Since his return, Laurette had done scarcely one full day's work, complaining it was not the place of a lady to undertake menial tasks usually performed by servants, even though she had to go without if she did not do them herself.

'Holly! Why, isn't it a pleasure to see her sitting down for a change, Richard? I do declare this girl will work herself into the ground if you do not take her in hand. Look how thin she is getting. And that hair? I swear Mimosa hasn't laid a brush on it in days,' Laurette said smilingly as she lowered herself into the nearest chair. 'Be a dear, and ring for Joseph. I must have something cold to drink.'

'Coffee, Joseph, and some lemonade for Miss Laurette. Coffee or brandy, Richard?' Holly refrained from commenting on the remarks as Joseph appeared behind her chair.

'Both. I had rather too much of that excellent claret with dinner last night. I must admit it made me feel very much at home.' Richard drew a chair towards him with a booted foot and sprawled into it in an untidy fashion. 'Bring some cigars, Joseph.'

'Those, like the claret, are fast running out,' Holly said coolly. 'In fact, last night's bottle was all we have. The Yankees emptied the cellar, and since you arrived, we have used up what was left.' Why did she make it sound like an accusation, she wondered? She knew the answer straight away. Before he came, everyone in the house worked hard for the meal they sat down to at night. Sometimes it was not much, at other times she allowed the use of preserved vegetables or a bottle of wine, or bottled fruit, as a treat. For her it always was. Something extra and very much appreciated. Since Richard's return she had come to realise how much she and everyone else in her family, and probably throughout the South, had taken so many things for granted. The negroes who worked for them, a good harvest which produced cotton in abundance and therefore money in the bank to maintain the standard of living to which they had always been accustomed. Despite all he had been through in the past four years, what he had seen and should have learned, Holly realised he was now as he had always been. How Clayton and Robert would be if they were here with her. Masters of everything they surveyed, expecting obedience, loyalty, devotion from those they employed. A woman to charm them with her wit, perhaps her beauty, but never her knowledge. In the South a woman was an ornament, without a mind of her own. Holly began to wonder if she would be able to survive in the old world were it suddenly available to her again.

She had obtained an independence of spirit that could not be suppressed. She had grown used to giving orders, had gained immense satisfaction from the knowledge which had come to her over these past years of the maintenance and handling of a plantation. It was not as difficult as men pretended. She was doing it, and successfully, under the most difficult of circumstances. She was mistress of Tanglewood now in her own right. For the first time she acknowledged it. Her father's death had made it so. He had bequeathed her a legacy she would never part with until the day she died.

'I've been thinking.' Richard waited until Joseph had departed again and he had helped himself to a large glass of brandy to accompany his coffee. 'You should sell this place, Holly. With the money from it, which wouldn't be very much unless you sold to someone outside the county, which is what I'm thinking of, you could come back to Atlanta with me. We could build a fine house there. The city is booming again now.'

Holly counted to ten, caught Laurette's eye on her, and drank a little coffee while she fought for her composure. Laurette would be all for that idea.

'I am sure you think that an excellent idea, but I shall never sell Tanglewood. I shall sell the cotton when it is ready and use the money to build the place up again,' she replied in a quiet, determined, tone.

'Build up the place? Sell the cotton? Good lord, girl, you won't harvest enough this year to pay your taxes,' came the scornful answer.

She stared into the face of the man she had once pledged to marry. The youthful face had become hard and lined with hardships she knew nothing about. But there was something else, too, something that made her uneasy. A disregard for those about him, as though no one existed but Richard Mitchell. The preservation of Richard Mitchell being of prime importance. She could understand his necessity to feel part of a family again, wanted, loved, even, but he had made no attempt to contact his parents, who had moved to relatives in Augusta after Sherman's devastation of Atlanta. He seemed at home only here, as though he had decided that here he would stay, no matter what! But this was *her* home, and she did not love him or wish to marry him. He could not stay! She experienced a sensation of near panic such as she had not known since the day Tanglewood had been abandoned to the Yankee soldiers. Suddenly she felt boxed in on all sides, as if she were being manipulated towards a goal not of her choosing.

Taxes. She had not considered those. Again the most

important issue was thrust to the back of her mind. She would broach it with him when they were alone.

'What taxes, Richard.'

'Cotton taxes, girl. What else?'

She coloured hotly. Why did he always have to speak to her as if she was an ignoramus.

'When did your father last pay cotton taxes for Tanglewood?'

She tried to recollect, and remembered something many years ago.

'He—he arranged with the bank, I think, to have money available. Until two years ago. I'm not sure.'

'Then you owe two years' back taxes—that's if the bank paid up for you. Don't forget the Confederate greenback is worthless now, and has been declining in value since 1862. It's possible that there was not enough to cover the demand. Don't you think you should go to see your bank manager?'

'I was in Savannah not long ago, but he said nothing then. Only that our savings are worthless.' She gave a hollow laugh and lowered her head into her hands. In doing so, she did not see the look which passed between Richard and Laurette. Standing just inside the doorway, Joseph did, and it was not the first time he had witnessed these furtive smiles. Without a doubt he knew a conspiracy was in the wind, and he turned away, shaking his grey-haired head in troubled silence. It was not his place to point the finger, but if he did not . . .

'Why don't we all go to Savannah for a few days? The break will do you good, Holly. The war's over. Let's have a little celebration. Let's go and see how much they are willing to offer us on this run-down wreck of a plantation,' Richard said, smiling across the table at her.

'You are right. I need to get away from here for a

while. It will make me more appreciative of what I have when I return.' Holly stood up, her voice like ice, containing the fury in her which made her want to strike out at his smiling face for his total lack of understanding. 'I shall see the bank manager again and try to arrange a loan. In two or three years I shall be able to repay it, I am sure. When that is settled, you and I must talk. We have things to say that are long overdue. Shall we say next week? Joseph and Joshua can manage for a few days without me.' She laid heavy emphasis on the last word, and Richard's brows rose sardonically, but he made no comment.

'It isn't going to be as easy as you think,' Laurette said quietly as Holly went inside. She gulped back some of his brandy and he refilled his glass, frowning.

'You will make it more difficult if you carry on in this way. Relax, my sweet, we have dear little Holly just where we want her.'

'And where is that?'

'Dangling. Dangling between the devil and the deep blue sea. One way she loses the plantation and goes to hell. The other she drowns. Either way, we shall be free of her.'

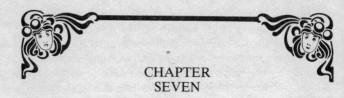

CHAPTER
SEVEN

'COME IN, Joshua, and shut the door. I must speak with you before we go.' Holly closed the ledger and locked it away in the desk before folding the paper on which was written vital figures and information. She had estimated that within eighteen months, or two years at the most, Tanglewood would have produced enough cotton, when sold, to repay the money she was going to ask from the bank for grain, seed, new wagons, and fresh hands to work the fields and get every one of them back into production again.

The tall negro hovered beside the desk. Holly had given him some of her brother's clothes, when his own had gone beyond repair. Robert had been a lean, gangling youth, nowhere as broad as Joshua, and the checked shirt, open to the waist, barely covered his chest. The sleeves, too short by inches, were rolled back over muscled arms. As she waited, she had been wondering how to approach him on the subject of his dismissal, and had come to the conclusion that she had no choice but to stand firm on what she believed to be right. 'Is everything ready?'

'The wagon is out front, Miz Holly.'

'I want you to come to Savannah with me.' Deliberately she omitted any reference to Richard. He was merely a guest in the house. *She* was mistress. 'I pray we shall be advanced a loan by the bank, and I shall need you to advise me on what we need so that the money is spent to its best advantage.'

'That ain't my job no more. Mr Richard, he's running the place for you now. I suppose that's only right, with you and him getting married and all,' Joshua said in a flat tone.

'You presume to know too much.' Holly rose stiffly to her feet. Folding her arms, she leaned back against the desk, angry sparks of fire in her eyes as she considered the ebony face before her. Not a flicker of emotion. He was Joseph's son, all right! Neither gave anything away. It was infuriating at times to know that she was constantly under surveillance and was unable, even for an instant, to determine the train of thought of whichever of them was studying her. 'When I tell everyone I am getting married, then you may accept it as fact. Also, when I tell you I no longer want you as my overseer, then you will go back to the fields, or leave, or whatever you please. You are a free man now. You have a choice in what you do.'

'Mimosa! One day that girl's loose tongue will be the death of her.'

'For once, I am glad of her chatter. I thought Mr Richard was being helpful. I had no idea what he had done, and would have remained ignorant for some considerable time, as it seemed that you were not willing to tell me. Or that you did not care enough that a position of trust I had given you was taken away—that you were ordered back to the fields like a common hand?'

Joshua shrugged broad shoulders.

'I was bought as a field hand. The work ain't as hard as trying to run the place.'

'I never thought you would be afraid of a challenge.' Why was it he always made her feel as if he were above her, Holly wondered. It was most disconcerting. It could not continue if they were to work together in the future.

The partnership would always make her uneasy, but in the eyes of the law, thanks to President Lincoln, all slaves were free and equal with their white masters. She felt a twinge of pity for all those thousands of negroes who had been flung, penniless, homeless, friendless, into a strange new world which offered them less, now that the war was over, than the promises had implied. Far less than many of them had had as slaves. 'You are not like some of the others, prepared to stay in the fields. There is ambition in you, Joshua, or you would have left with the Yankees. I don't know what you have in mind, or your dreams, your hopes. I only know what mine are. To get this place back on its feet, and I cannot do it alone. I want you as my overseer. I need you.'

For a moment only, jet black eyes registered surprise, and then a faint smile touched the man's mouth. 'I'll stay. My pa's happy here and I am, too. If 'n I'm a free man now, does that mean I can take me a woman without asking your permission?'

'You don't need mine, but I rather think you will need Mimosa's,' Holly replied.

'She'll do as I say, or I'll put her over my knee. About time someone took a hand with that girl. You approve, then?'

'I am sure she will make you a good wife.'

'She will give me many fine sons. Free sons. This will be a good place for them to be raised.'

His words took away Holly's breath. He was making long-term plans.

'I—I can't pay you, you realise that, don't you? Not yet, anyway. If I get this loan, there will be little to spare except for essentials like work-clothes and food. I won't be able to pay anyone regular wages until we are back on our feet again. I estimate two years.'

'My figuring, too.' Joshua nodded. There was a new

look in his eyes as he considered the slim girl before him. If she had not been so sure of his dislike for her, Holly would have believed it to be admiration. 'Cotton crop's only half of what it should be this year. With a new barn, a wagon, new team and some help, we'll be as good as new by then. My mammy was right, God rest her soul. She said you were a fighter. Right about the trouble comin' your way, too.'

'Trouble?' Holly echoed. 'What are you talking about?'

'Reckon now is as good a time as any to tell you. You're in the middle of it right now, as far as I can see. When she was dying, my mammy made me promise her I'd stay on here and take care of you. Folks were right when they said she had "second sight". She saw trouble ahead for you, Miz Holly. She was afraid for you all alone.'

Holly remembered with affection, and with a longing for those large comforting arms, the woman who had raised her from childhood. A servant, friend, adviser and, at times, a veritable dragon when it came to controlling the high spirits that accompanied those carefree days when she and her brothers rampaged through the plantation in search of ways to alleviate their boredom in the long, lazy, hot days with nothing to do.

'She knew I would be alone?' Holly looked at Joshua with new respect. 'You have done everything she asked of you. I am in no danger, now the war is over. You can leave, if you wish, knowing you have kept the promise made to her.'

'It ain't that easy. My going away ain't going to change nothing,' the man declared. 'Bad things is going to happen here. Have happened. The Yankees were only the beginning.'

Holly paled, but stayed in control of the fear which

flickered through her like a blast of icy wind. He sounded so sure of himself. Bad things! What kind of things? Tanglewood was safe, despite Major Jared Ruell and his vicious orders which had almost destroyed them all.

'You had better stay close to me then, Joshua. I need fear no one with you at my back. I've changed, have I not? Mistress, and yet no longer mistress of this place. Not as before, anyway.'

'You will always be mistress of Tanglewood, Miz Holly. There ain't anyone going to take that right away from you. 'Cept maybe . . .'

She looked at him sharply, her keen instincts immediately picking up his line of thought.

'Richard? I am going to ask him to leave, the moment we return from Savannah. It seems we are both of one mind. His parents' home was destroyed when the Yankees went through Atlanta, and his parents are with relatives now. I thought it strange he did not want to go and see them. He cannot stay any longer. We—there will be no marriage between us.'

'Pa figured that when he saw his eyes straying elsewhere.'

Laurette! It had to be, there was nobody else. Married to Holly, he would be in control of the plantation and have the mistress of his choice as well. The deviousness of men would never fail to amaze her. 'He ain't no loss to you, not like the other one,' Joshua added matter-of-factly, and she flushed.

Holly reached for her shawl and pulled on the last pair of white gloves she possessed, biting back an icy retort. Had everyone noticed her stupidity?

Laurette and Richard were coming downstairs as Holly and Joshua emerged from the study. Instantly her sister-in-law disengaged herself. Joshua was right. It had been happening under her very nose, and she had been too preoccupied to notice it. Trying to heal the wound of her father's death by more work, determined not to allow herself to be dragged down once again into the dismal pit of depression in which Jared had left her, and from which she had only recently escaped. She had been blind!

'I'm sorry I was so long, Holly dear.' Laurette bestowed a smile on her as she drew closer. 'I couldn't find a decent thing to wear. I see you had the same trouble.' Her gaze fastened on Holly's black dress, usually worn only on occasions of mourning. 'Or are you expecting a refusal on the part of your bank manager?'

'I have learned never to expect anything,' Holly replied coolly. 'Good morning, Richard.'

He leaned forward and lightly brushed her mouth with his.

'Don't worry. Everything will be all right. Just leave everything to me,' he assured her. His words brought Holly no comfort.

'That is very kind of you, but Tanglewood is my responsibility and I would not dream of burdening you with its troubles.' Holly's eyes fastened on the grey broadcloth suit he wore, and she caught her breath. 'What are you doing in Clayton's clothes? How dare you!'

'I gave them to him,' Laurette declared in a voice that defied argument. 'I may do what I please with my husband's clothes, Holly. Besides, poor Richard could hardly accompany us looking like a "cracker", could he? You have given some of Robert's cast-offs to Joshua, I see. You will be giving him ideas above his station with your generosity.'

'As overseer of Tanglewood, Joshua also has a position to uphold.'

'Just a minute!' Richard's face creased into a scowl.
'I dismissed him. He's insolent and untrustworthy. I
won't have him near me.'

'Must I remind you, Richard, that you are a guest in
my house. Nothing more,' Holly answered, bracing
herself for the confrontation she had tried desperately
to avoid. 'I did not want to speak of this to you until
we came back, nor in front of an audience, but as you
have raised the matter . . . Our engagement is at an
end. It was foolish of us ever to have thought we could
be happy together, but we were young and I—I was
very foolish. I do not deny that. As we are no longer to
be married, you must realise you cannot remain here
any longer.'

'Leave? Holly, you aren't serious!' Richard's tone
was shocked as he contemplated the ruination of all his
carefully made plans. Damn Laurette's possessiveness.
Holly had realised what was going on between them.
How long had he got? A week, perhaps two if he was
cunning? 'My dear, I realise we have been little more
than strangers since I came back, but that was to be
expected. We hardly knew each other before I went
away.' He took her hand and pressed it to his lips,
unaware of the shudder she barely suppressed. 'It is my
fault. All of it. I have been thoughtless to expect us to
be able to pick up the threads as though the war had
never happened. Poor Holly, you never did have a real
courtship. That's what you want, isn't it? To be wooed
all over again, the way it should have been?'

'Richard, no,' she protested. How persuasive he could
be when he wished. Looking into his open gaze, she
found it hard to believe there was a liaison between
himself and Laurette until she turned slightly and noticed the warning look on Joshua's face. 'It won't work.
Please don't make this difficult for us.'

'We shall talk of it when we come home again,' he said softly, and the face was suddenly as she remembered it. Young, boyish, wiped clean of all lines, smiling at her as he had done that day beneath the rose arbour when he had said he loved her. Her, or the prospect of becoming master of Tanglewood after her father's death, she wondered miserably? Why did he have to prolong the inevitable? 'If you are still sure I have no place in your life . . .' Again his lips touched her fingers, slid over the back of her hand in a silken caress. 'Then I shall leave. But I want us to try, Holly. Give me three weeks. It will be as it was before I went away, I promise.'

'Three weeks will make no difference to the way I feel, but . . .' Holly capitulated. 'Very well. Shall we go? Joshua?'

'She knows,' Laurette hissed, hanging back as Holly and the negro went outside. 'What are we going to do?'

'You are going to contain that very voracious appetite, my sweet, until I have things my way. I've been planning this for too long to have you ruin my prospect of owning this place.'

'You cold-blooded swine. Have you been thinking of this . . .'

'Ever since I first laid eyes on her. Of course I didn't think I would wind up with Tanglewood at first, but with all the men gone . . . She needs me.'

'She has that negro. Did you see the way he was watching her. Almost . . . almost . . . I found it quite disgusting. He is in her confidence, you realise that.' She was beside herself with rage. Just when things seemed to be going their way, Holly had to get a fit of self-righteous conscience.

'Within three weeks I guarantee that Holly Beaufort will be eating out of my hand.'

'You still plan to marry her? I won't let you! Not now.'

'You will do as I say. No, I don't intend marrying her, not that I've any qualms about taking her down a peg or two before I've finished with her. Bedding with a Yankee! I didn't think her tastes ran as low as yours. I have another ace up my sleeve, my angel. If I play it right, I shall have everything I want. Money—lots of money . . . enough to keep me and you in comfort for a very long time. Before the war I had planned to marry Holly and settle here. The life would have been good, and I should have lived in a style to which I could have become accustomed, as you have, very quickly. It's different now. I've seen too much death and squalor. I'm not fighting any more for anyone but myself, and I'm not going to live on anyone else's charity. I don't have the money to put this place back on its feet. It would be a millstone around my neck if I married Holly now. I have different plans. If I'm not mistaken, and I'm going to verify my facts in Savannah, I can get this place when it comes up for back taxes, about September, maybe later. Then, anyone I don't want around the place goes. I'll have to borrow the money to do it, of course, but whoever lends it to me will be paid back double when I sell the place to some carpetbagger from the North looking for a real Southern plantation with which to impress his friends.'

'You would turn her out of here?' Laurette's eyes gleamed at the thought.

'One woman here will be sufficient. If you want to stay with me, that is?'

'Of course I do. You know I love you.' She ignored the cynical twist to his mouth at her words. 'Are you sure about the taxes? She will have some money from the cotton, remember.'

'Unless something happens to it before it can be sold.'
Richard turned and looked slowly around him. 'I shall
get good money for this place. Not as much as if it were
productive, of course, but I don't intend to be greedy.
Once the mortgage is paid, it will all be mine. What do
you think of a trip to France, my dear?'

Holly came out of the bank, biting back the tears which
threatened to rise. For the past hour, she had been
pleading to no avail, for money. She had stormed, railed
at the intransigence of the stony-faced bank manager
whom her father had once considered a friend, whose
eyes held no compassion or sympathy for her impossible
position. Mr Cauldwell's voice again and again condemned Tanglewood to bankruptcy. No loan! She had
no collateral. Nothing to bargain with. He did not
consider the small amount of cotton she had produced
worth even discussing.

Richard, for all the harsh words that had passed
between them before they left, had begged to be allowed
to accompany her, and at the last moment she had
relented. Perhaps he had a spark of feeling for her after
all, or was his concern only for Tanglewood and what
he would lose if it was sold? If she lost it, then he lost,
too. Even Laurette had insisted on accompanying them.
A show of force might turn the tide in their favour, she
insisted, adding, more in character, Holly had thought
bitterly, that she was in the process of losing a roof over
her head.

They had both remained behind, determined,
Richard assured her, to try and make the manager
change his mind. A few weeks' grace to try and borrow
the money elsewhere. Anything to keep them going
until the cotton was sold. Everything depended on that
small amount of cotton, Holly thought. She would sell

it as soon as it was harvested. If it could not pay all the taxes, it would at least show that she was making an effort. So long as she could keep the plantation, she had the will to work and keep it going. Keep herself going.

'You all right, Miz Holly?' Joshua asked as he helped her into the wagon. She was aware of the curious stares being directed her way. It should have been a fine carriage drawn by two strutting horses with gleaming coats instead of a worn, creaking wagon used for hauling vegetables from the fields. Let them stare! Her head went back proudly and Joshua climbed up into his place, his face averted so that she would not see the pride in him also. He was not free. Lincoln's decree, however well meaning, could never make him that. Perhaps for his children, and their children, it would be different. Here and now nothing had changed. He was a black servant driving his mistress. For him that feeling would never change, except that now it had taken on a new meaning. There was trust between them and friendship. The relationship made him in awe of her, afraid to step over the unseen boundaries which still separated them, knowing how much care must be taken with each step. It was the same for her, he realised, and so forgave her any sharpness of tongue, any note in her voice that made her the mistress and him still the slave. It had begun to change. It was how his mammy had predicted.

Behind him he heard Holly draw in her breath as if in alarm. He turned to look at her, asking, 'Is anything wrong? Shall I drive on or wait for the others?'

'Nothing. It's nothing.'

Her voice was faint, as though she were barely aware of his presence. Her gaze was focused on a horseman turning into the next street. A well-built man astride a bay mare. Joshua felt the muscles in his neck constrict.

He knew the horse immediately. Her horse! She had
recognised it, too, and its rider. As the man disappeared
from sight, she closed her eyes and sat rigid in her seat,
her hands locked tightly together in her lap. He cursed
the man who had once again brought her pain. After a
moment she seemed to recover.

'Mr Richard and Miss Laurette are still with Mr
Cauldwell. Trying to make him change his mind, I
think.' A vain hope and probably untrue. At last she
acknowledged Joshua was right. Richard wanted Tanglewood and through her, had they married, he would
have gained control. Never! She had watched them in
the small office. Laurette could scarcely contain her
pleasure at the forthcoming foreclosure. Richard, more
adept at hiding his feelings, probably because of the
war, gave nothing away. Yet she had sensed a growing
excitement in him at the news that she was not to receive
any money, despite his ardent speech on her behalf.
Excitement and satisfaction. Why? She still had control,
and would continue to have it once the cotton was
sold. She was anticipating something which would not
happen. In three weeks he would be gone. It was as
simple as that! On the way back to the hotel, she
convinced herself that she had not seen Jared Ruell,
merely somebody bearing a close resemblance. What
would he be doing in Savannah, anyway, and in civilian
clothes?

'Jared! I was expecting you two hours ago.' David Ruell
rose from behind his desk as his brother entered his
office. 'Late night, entertaining company, or both?'

'A profitable evening and a hangover,' Jared returned
dryly. 'I need a hair of the dog.'

Smiling, his brother turned from the decanter of
whiskey and held out a full glass to him.

'Drink that and then we can get down to business, although the news I have for you isn't what you want. I'm sorry.'

'Tell me, and then I'll tell you if you should be sorry.' Jared relaxed into a vacant chair. He liked David's office. It was pleasantly furnished, comfortably so, with an adequate supply of liquor and the company he missed so dearly during most of the hours of the day. He drank too much these days, he thought, and instantly dismissed the self-condemnation. He had reason enough.

'I received a letter from home this morning. Father died two days ago. I shall go back, of course, for the funeral.' David waited a moment, hoping for some reaction, even for a suggestion that Jared, too, would return, but his brother remained impassive, his concentration centred on the savouring of his drink. He knew it was to cover the shock he had received, and so forgave him his irreverence. 'You know of course, that Father has left everything to me . . . I mean, after what happened . . .'

Jared raised his head as David's voice tailed off into an uncomfortable silence. 'Don't be shy about saying it, Davie. I was dishonourably discharged from the army for disobeying an order in time of war. I ruined, deliberately, a fine career. Father could not understand, or accept that. The army was his life. He did not want to acknowledge a son who turned his back on everything he cherished. Don't feel bad about what happened. I don't. I'm glad he still had you to depend on. He thought he was doing the right thing and, by doing so, retained his self-respect. At the time I thought I was right, too, so we shall both end up in heaven, won't we?'

'Don't try the cynical routine with me, Jared, it won't work. You are as sad over his death as I am. More so. You were his favourite son, and no matter what happened between you, you loved him.'

'Damn you! Do you always have to strip me bare? It's indecent!' Jared declared, swallowing his drink without appreciation. Putting the glass to one side, he looked across at David and smiled, but his eyes were dark with pain.

'So I am still penniless, and you are rich and the head of a profitable law firm. Congratulations!'

'I've reserved a table for us at Michelle's for noon,' David said, naming one of the most expensive and most frequented restaurants in Savannah. Everyone who was someone, had been someone, before the war or wanted to be someone in the new order which was arising in the South, went there. 'We shall eat heartily, and get very drunk. I've taken the afternoon off and the evening as well. I'm coming home with you tonight. You may have to put me to bed as you did all those other times I got drunk and Father blamed you. Why did you always take the blame for me, Jared?'

'Perhaps I hoped he would make you his favourite son and let me out of West Point,' Jared joked without humour to accompany the words. David winced, and instantly he was contrite. 'Sorry, I didn't mean that. Have you any other news for me?'

'Oh, you mean that plantation you asked after? It's in a bad way, like most of them. In a few months—three, four at the most— it will probably be sold for taxes.'

Jared's mouth tightened visibly and his brother wondered what had taken place at this Southern plantation to make him desire it so vehemently. Jared produced a silver case and lit a long cheroot. His brother did not smoke, but never complained of the evil black cigars he smoked continually.

'Buy it for me,' he said, shutting down the veil over

that part of his mind that still retained the memory of Holly Beaufort. Bitch! She would soon discover that the spoils of war were going to cost her dear indeed!

'It could go for four, maybe five hundred. It's hard to say. I didn't go into an assessment of the place. Do you want me to?'

'Yes. I want it, no matter what I have to pay. I'll sell the house and the boat if necessary. Get it for me, David.'

By late August, the cotton was ready to harvest. The weather had been continually hot all month and the fleecy white bolls looked as good as they had ever done. Holly took the bit between her teeth and ordered the crop to be picked. By September she could pay the back taxes on Tanglewood. It was safe, yet again! For the first time since the war had disturbed the peace of her world, she heard the sound of singing as the negroes moved along the lines of cotton, plucking the flowers that were to bring them fresh security and hope for the future. Her heart sang too. She was winning!

Richard had left the house early in July, without argument or the scene she had been dreading when she still refused to renew their engagement. She had been too elated by his departure to suspect any ulterior motive in the sudden exit. Laurette had sulked for a week, then suddenly she, too, had become more considerate and helpful, as though she had cast off all shadows of the past and begun anew. She listened avidly to Holly's plans for the future, the reconstruction of destroyed or old buildings, new livestock and had even added her own suggestions. Holly could not have been more delighted. In the weeks which followed, her natural dislike of her sister-in-law, and the betrayal of the dead brother she had adored, were put to the back of her mind in an attempt to find common ground between them to build a foundation for the future. Their future. Only Joshua stayed in the background, neither condemning nor aiding her attempts at reconciliation. She thought this was because Laurette still treated him as a field hand, and his resentment over this would never fade. In time, she hoped, they would become not friends but allies against a continual war of survival. Every hand was needed. Even Joseph, in his late sixties, worked with them like a man of forty and never complained. Mimosa, since she and Joshua had become united, never uttered a word of reproach against her mistress or anyone in the house, where she used to be the first to point the finger at a lazy negro, a listener at keyholes or a chatterbox, forgetful of her own loose tongue.

September was a wonderful month. The barn was three-quarters full of cotton, soon to be shipped to Savannah. She would be paid in Yankee gold, but it did not matter. What should matter except that she still retained possession of Tanglewood?

Holly awoke to the sound of screaming and hoarse shouts of horror, and thrust aside the bedclothes, still fogged with sleep. The Yankees were coming again! No, that was not possible. The war was over. How many times had she had the same dream. Flames licking hungrily around the barns, the precious cotton, the only wealth Tanglewood possessed. Lieutenant Rhys, sneering at her as he threw in another torch. Jared, leading her best horses off into the distance. How many times since had she levelled the Derringer at him and pulled the trigger? One day she would make him pay. One day soon, she told herself when waking from another nightmare, her nightgown soaked with perspir-

ation, she would settle with him and restore her peace
of mind.

'Send everyone out into the fields tomorrow,' Holly
had told Joshua that evening. She was jubilant. One
more day would see the picking finished. Then would
come the sale and badly-needed money. 'We are almost
there.'

Almost, the negro thought, but not quite. Why did
he feel this terrible premonition of disaster? What could
happen to them now? They were almost home!

What had happened *was* a fire. The most terrible
disaster of all. Flames again, and real this time, Holly
realised, as she struggled into a robe. The cotton!
No! Not again! It was her nightmare. Nothing more
than that, but as she ran outside and saw the black
figures hauling water in continuous buckets towards
the barn that Joshua had only just finished repairing,
her heart sank. With that feeling of despair that crept
into her heart came the realisation that there was
nothing she could do. Without the cotton, there would
be no money to pay the taxes. Weeping, she sank on
to the veranda steps. Joshua, coming to enlist what
help still remained at the house, bit back the angry
words which rose to his lips at the sight of her dejected
figure, and passed her by, threatening dire retribution
for anyone who did not carry a full bucket to the
flames. From where she sat, Holly watched the roof
once more collapse in a sheet of bright flame, gathered
her robe about her, and went back to her room. It
was finished. She was finished!

Hours later, as she watched the smouldering ashes
from the window, Joshua came to tell her that two of
the field hands had disappeared, and he suspected that
they had been paid to start the blaze. Holly shrugged.
What did it matter now, who had started it, or why?

There was nothing she could do any more. The last of her strength had been consumed in the flames. She did not even have enough left to shed a tear.

'What did she say?' Joseph asked as his son returned to the kitchen and sank wearily into a chair.

'She wasn't interested. There ain't nothing she can do to raise the tax money, and she knows it.'

'Did you tell her what you suspected?'

'That Miz Laurette paid the two runaways to do it? What would be the use? We ain't got no proof.'

'That woman and Mr Richard are up to something. They've been carrying on ever since he came back.'

'Up to what? She ain't got no money to pay the taxes, no more than he. Both of them been living off Miz Holly. If anyone's to blame for all this, it's that Yankee Major. Don't look at me like that, I know you liked him. Don't see how you still can, after what he did to her and this place. You should have seen him! On her horse, all dressed up in fine clothes, silk shirt, no less. Got himself rich from robbing and burning. One day soon I'm going back to Savannah to find him and, when I do, I'm going to kill him.'

Holly tore up the summons for payment of back taxes which arrived by messenger early in September, did not attend the court hearing, or move one inch from the house for over two weeks after she knew Tanglewood no longer belonged to her. She knew she had to accept it, but she did not know how.

'Hello, Holly.' Richard sat smiling at her from his horse as she sat on the veranda, still desperately seeking an avenue of escape, and knowing in her heart it was too late. 'I hear you have had some bad luck. Not to worry, I won't insist on your leaving just yet, providing you remember your manners.'

Holly remembered staring at him for a long while until his words sank into her, and their meaning spelled doom for her and all the negroes who had so steadfastly maintained her throughout her period of tribulation. Richard would get rid of them, cast them out to fend for themselves, unless they promised to obey his every word. Lincoln had changed the South. He had not changed men like Richard Mitchell.

'I have bought Tanglewood, Holly.' The smile on his face made her want to scream. Laurette came out to join him. Side by side they faced her. It had always been that way, she acknowledged. Now she knew that the child Laurette had lost would not have been her brother's. Those months in Atlanta where Richard was garrisoned before Sherman marched through, and in Savannah before he left to march deep into the interior of North Carolina. Lovers! They had been then, as they were now. He had never belonged to her—and she had reproached herself for her lack of feeling. Holly rose from her chair like an old woman. It was the way she felt.

'I shall not stay,' she declared, and he shrugged his shoulders.

'We do not want you,' Laurette said cattily. 'The sooner you leave the better, and take that insolent Joshua with you, and Joseph, too, and anyone else you want. We shall buy new servants.'

'I pity them,' was all Holly said before she turned and went inside.

'Richard and I are married, you know.' Laurette's voice halted her as she reached the stairs. 'Last week. I am mistress here now, Holly. Not you.'

Damn your Southern pride, Jared had once said to her. It was all she possessed to convey her to her room, to close and lock the door behind her before she collapsed across her bed in a fit of weeping that Mimosa, when she found her mistress an hour later, could not stem. In anxiety, she went in search of Joseph. Not even he managed to halt the flow of tears, the recriminations she poured down on her own head for her failure to see what was happening under her very nose. It was Joshua who came to her by a back way, sat beside the bed, and talked to her in quiet tones that somehow found their way into her stunned brain. Tanglewood was not lost while Holly Beaufort was alive, he told her, and, as the night wore on, she began to believe it. It no longer belonged to her, yet it was still hers. It was her inheritance from grandfather Lucien.

She gave her orders a week later, and Mimosa obeyed without a word of protest. After dark, eight days after Tanglewood had passed into the hands of Richard Mitchell, Joshua harnessed a pair of horses, made ready the wagons with blankets, the trunk packed with Holly's scant belongings and with her seated beside him, hugging a woollen shawl about her body, Joseph and Mimosa behind them, they left. In the house the new owner and his wife were celebrating their victory in the dining-room, both of them more than a little drunk at their success.

Holly steeled herself not to look back, knowing the pain it would cause, but she could not help herself. At the last bend in the drive before the house disappeared from sight, unaware that Jared had similarly looked back, she turned and gazed over her shoulder. The house was ablaze with lights. Where Richard had obtained the money for such extravagance she did not know, any more than she could puzzle out the source from which he had obtained money to pay the back taxes. With a stifled sob, she averted her gaze and fought to keep back the tears.

'Drive on, Joshua,' she whispered to the silent figure at her side. 'Let us be gone from here.'

'I'm sorry, Jared. It all happened so quickly. I smell some collusion somewhere. I had scarcely begun my approaches to the bank that is handling the plantation affairs, when Cauldwell, the manager, told me it had been sold for taxes. I did warn you that this could happen,' David added. 'This kind of thing has been happening frequently since the end of the war. Speculators flocking in from the North.'

'Eager to make their fortunes by the misfortunes of others,' Jared remarked bitterly. 'Human nature disgusts me at times. So there's nothing I can do?'

'On the contrary, we are by no means out of the running. The new owner is making overtures to businessmen and such like. He does not care where they come from apparently, as long as they are willing to pay the price he asks for the place in Yankee dollars.'

'Who bought it?' Jared asked stiffly. Tanglewood sold—*She* would never have allowed it!

'Wait a minute.' David sifted through a mass of papers on his desk. 'Mitchell. Richard Mitchell. What is it?' He looked up startled as his brother swore. 'You know him?'

'Of him. She hasn't lost the place. It's been taken over, that's all. The fiancé is back from the war. Welcomed with open arms, by the look of it.'

'He and his wife are still in residence. Richard and Laurette Mitchell. I thought the girl who owned the place was Holly Beaufort? That was the name, wasn't it?'

'The sister-in-law. My God! He's married that whore Rhys bedded.'

David looked disapprovingly across the papers. He did not like his brother when he was in one of these

moods. Despite their closeness, there were times when
Jared was so distant from him, untouchable. 'I bet she's
humbled now. Come on, I'll buy you lunch.'

'What is this? A celebration?' David smiled.

Jared rose from his chair, his face unsmiling.

'A wake for someone I used to know.'

Over lunch and some excellent wine, he began to
talk. David listened, and did not like what he heard:
the venom which came into his brother's tone at the
mention of the same plantation, the same woman. But
he listened, because he had never known Jared to be
so much involved with a woman before that it marred
his judgment, controlled his life, as it seemed to be
doing now. Jared in love? It was just possible. Jared
humiliated, perhaps betrayed. That was certain, or he
would not be acting this way.

They ate well, as they always did when they went out
together. As they drank coffees and brandies, Jared
looked across the table and asked, 'How much do you
think the plantation is worth?'

'A great deal more than you have to offer,' David
returned good-humouredly. 'As it is at the moment, it's
not worth any more than was paid for it, but when it
gets back into full production . . . You can't afford it,
Jared, not even if you sell the boat and the house.'

'Estimate their worth, and then tell me again.'

'You are really serious, aren't you? From what I've
seen on paper it's quite a place, but then you were
there, you know that.'

'Offer them whatever you think is enough to whet
their appetite. I want it, David, no matter what the
cost.'

'Good lord, man, you don't have that kind of money.'

'I'll borrow it.' The quiet voice was unnervingly confident.

'What is it you want so badly?' David asked, lighting his brother's cigar. 'The plantation, or the woman?'

'That's my business.' Jared scowled at him, but did not rise to the taunt.

'You are making it mine by involving me in all this. I'm not sure I like what is driving you. I've never seen you so preoccupied before over anyone—or anything. She must be something special.'

'When I've finished with her, she'll be glad to crawl into the nearest hole and hide,' Jared returned brutally. 'She's going to learn what it's like to crawl, as I once did. To lose everything dear to them, as I did. Have it destroyed by . . . I move among a society that thinks itself better than me, when in fact I walk ten feet taller than any of them with their false values. She was like that. She once told me that her Southern pride was all she had left. Well, this Yankee is going to take that from her.'

'My God,' David ejaculated. 'I thought you cared for the girl?'

'Cared? There was something, for a short time, but she destroyed it. She sent me away with her death-curse ringing in my ears. Care! I'll see her damned first! If you don't have the stomach for any of this, I'll find someone else.'

'I'll do what I can,' David said, signalling to the waiter to bring their bill. 'I don't agree with what you are doing, but I know you are hurt, Jared. I'll do it because of that. You are my brother.'

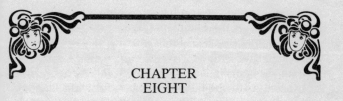

CHAPTER
EIGHT

It was three days before Holly managed to find a suitable place to stay in Savannah. The city was overloaded with refugees from places such as Macon, Augusta, Columbia. Some had lost their homes and all they possessed and were now crowding together in poverty-stricken hovels which often lacked the most primitive comforts. Huge families lived in one small room and were charged an exorbitant rent for the pleasure of a roof over their heads. The best houses and rooms had long since been taken by Union soldiers, many of whom still remained to garrison the city and restore order for the forthcoming elections.

Order, Holly thought in bewilderment and dismay as she trudged from house to house vainly seeking accommodation. The whole place was in chaos. Black faces stared at her everywhere she went, and she was pretty sure that only the continual presence of either Joshua or Joseph by her side prevented her from being accosted. It was a common happening in the streets, so she heard. In some parts of Savannah, a white face was immediate reason enough to storm and rampage through the streets, attacking anyone in sight. From what she could see, the blue-coats who had liberated them did nothing, and often looked on with amusement as yet another Southern man or woman was set upon. Negroes lounged on the sidewalk, in store doorways, making no move to step aside when she tried to pass, forcing her into the street to avoid them.

Speculators and 'carpetbaggers', as the new arrivals were called—for they arrived in a new place with only one such bag, intending to reap full benefit from Southern misfortunes, which many did within a short time—took up the remainder of the vacant rooms in hotels and boarding-houses. Holly had no cash in hand and was forced to sell, piece by piece, the small amount of jewellery she had brought with her. She received only a quarter of what it was worth, but she was thankful to have enough Yankee notes in her purse to buy food for them all.

At last she found two rooms on the edge of the city, in the house of a woman widowed in the war. She had lost a husband, two brothers and a son, and her circumstances were so reduced that she was forced to take in sewing from a local dressmaking shop, now booming to make gowns in the latest fashions brought by Northern women into Savannah. Until Holly's arrival, she had refused to accept boarders, but after one look at the ashen-faced girl being supported by a huge negro on her doorstep, she quickly ushered them inside. Her original intention was to offer them nothing more than a hot drink and a meal, but as the day wore on, and Joshua in no uncertain terms told her what had befallen Holly and led to her state of near collapse, the woman's mood changed. Holly could have a room in the house, and the other three could use an outhouse to sleep in.

When Holly awoke, however, she would not hear of being separated from the people who were fast becoming staunch friends, who had left a comfortable existence to remain at her side. Eventually she came to an agreement with the woman, whose name was Martha Daniels.

She would pay for a room for herself, and a smaller one at the back of the house for her companions. In return for being near her, they would do work around the house to earn their keep. That night, for the first time since leaving Tanglewood, she slept fitfully. Not until the morning when she opened her trunk and began to unpack her clothes and, for the first time since leaving Tanglewood, examined the contents of her jewel-box to ascertain how long her precious funds would last, did she discover the last and cruellest trick fate had placed on her. Richard or Laurette, probably both in collusion, had ransacked the contents. Most of her grandmother's heirlooms were missing, and also sentimental trinkets left to her by her mother. All that remained were a few rings and bracelets of no great value. Beneath these were valueless baubles belonging to Laurette. She did not tell the others. She could not tell them.

She hated to see the last of September slip away. Once it had been her favourite month for it had meant long days out of doors picnicking, watching the cotton being harvested. There was always a huge ball at the house when it had all been picked. However hard she tried not to think of the past, it came back time and time again to remind her of what she had lost, and what had been stolen from her. Mimosa, strangely without protest, helped around the house and often did the cooking when Martha was busy sewing late. Holly learned to cook, too, although her hands bore more blisters and cuts from failed attempts than successes. She continued to lose weight, for she ate sparingly, conscious of her dwindling resources. Cautiously she bought materials and sat sewing with her new friend at night, making blouses and skirts for herself and Mimosa, shirts for the two men. Joshua went out to earn what he could doing odd jobs, but work was hard to find.

Joseph, too old to do heavy labour any longer, kept house with the same meticulous care as he had at Tanglewood. Had she wished to boast to her neighbours, Martha Daniels could have told them that despite her lack of money, she had her meals cooked for her, the house swept and cleaned from top to bottom every day, and her clothes laundered. And she had the company of a genteel young lady who, like so many other Southern women, now lived in drastically reduced circumstances.

'Martha, I really must do more to help with our keep,' Holly said, as the two women sat drinking coffee late one afternoon. 'I have only one thing left to sell. When the money from that, too, has been spent, I shall have to leave here unless I can find some way of earning a living. Oh, I am so hopeless. What was I trained for? How to entertain guests, lay a fine table, what food to eat, wines to drink. What cigars to give the men. I am useless in this world!'

'I won't listen to you talk about yourself like that.' Martha reached across from her chair and took one of Holly's hands in hers, examining the new blister on the palm. 'You try hard enough. It isn't your fault. Hands like this were not made for the rough work you do.' She was a woman in her late thirties, but she looked nearer fifty. Hair, once brown, was already heavily streaked with grey. Her face was lined. Only the eyes remained young and always smiling. Looking into them, Holly felt ashamed at her lack of stamina and courage. 'I wanted to die when I received the news that my son, only fifteen, had been killed in the last bloody fighting around Richmond, but some of us have to fight on, Holly dear. Don't despair. God hasn't forsaken you. This is a test, and I know you will survive it and triumph.'

'I wish I had your faith,' Holly whispered, clutching tightly to the hand that held hers and gaining comfort from the strong grip. She was like a rock, but she would not be there for ever. She must not allow herself to use this fine, brave woman as a crutch any longer. 'Do you think I could get work as a seamstress? I embroider well and my stitching is neat.'

'I should think Ada—Madame Ada as she calls herself since the rich men and their fancy women arrived —would be pleased to take you on. I'll give you her address, and you take yourself off right now and see her. Tell her you are staying with me.' The address safely in her pocket, and with strict orders not to accept less than the sum Martha had told her she herself was earning, Holly set off into town accompanied by Joshua. It was the first time she had been outside the door in almost two weeks, apart from shopping at the near-by market. It was a warm, pleasant afternoon and she felt her cares slipping away from her for a moment at least. She looked straight ahead as she walked, ignoring the rude glances of the negroes lounging on the sidewalks. Colouring, but maintaining a dignified silence as blue-uniformed figures tossed invitations her way, as if she was one of those women! An hour later, she emerged from Madame Ada's shop with a promise of work for as long as the orders continued to come in. A little bartering had been necessary over the wage, but Holly had insisted on the rate that Martha had told her, and, to her delight, that was the rate settled for in the end. Holly Beaufort, seamstress! Making beautiful gowns for other women to wear, never wearing them herself! Those times were gone for ever. If only she could reconcile herself to the fact, Tanglewood was also gone for ever.

In the weeks that followed, she discovered that her needlework, which she had considered above average and had brought her compliments from all her friends at home, did not come up to the required standard. For several days she was reduced to tears as her work was rejected as unsatisfactory, and had to be unpicked and redone. She sat up until the early hours of the morning, refusing Martha's offer of assistance as she knew very well that she had more than her fair share of work to cope with, until she had caught up on the back-log of dresses and they had all been accepted. Only then did she receive any money. When she had bought food and other necessities and paid Martha, she would have nothing left. Reluctantly she went to the closet where she kept her clothes and belongings, and took out from an old glove the last remaining piece of jewellery worth selling. A signet ring belonging to her father, set with a perfect single diamond. When it had gone, she would have only her sewing-money with which to support herself and her three companions. It would never be enough!

She remembered Madame Ada's sly suggestion that, with her looks and figure, she would make more money if she took employment at one of the houses which provided entertainment for the gentlemen of the city. Holly's cheeks had burned with angry colour, and with a toss of her head she had stalked from the shop, the woman's laughter ringing in her ears.

'Take it and sell it for me,' she said, as she put the ring into Joshua's hand. 'Please try to get a good price.'

'I'll try somewhere new. Those big houses over on Greenbank Avenue. I've heard there's gambling over there. Plenty of money. Don't you worry none, Miz Holly. I'll get good money for it but, if I don't, I might just take what's owed us.'

'You will do no such thing,' Holly reproved, and for a moment he caught a glimpse of the mistress he had once known. He looked contrite and said he would not, but he had no intention of keeping the promise. He would do whatever was necessary to put food in their mouths and keep a roof over their heads. Looking at it logically, if he robbed the Yankees and 'carpetbaggers', he was only taking back what had been stolen from them all in the first place. As Joseph watched his son leave the house, his lined face was full of pride.

'Why does she look so pleased with herself?' Mimosa hissed, as she watched Holly sit down in the rocker and take up her sewing again. 'That work ain't going to keep us, is it? Look at her. Half asleep, she is. That dress won't be finished by tomorrow.'

'It might be, if you'd lend a hand. If you don't care to, then get on with your other work and hold your tongue,' Joseph rebuked in a low whisper. 'She's doing everything she can to keep us together. Lawd knows, there's no reason why she should care about us now. Without us, she'd stand a chance. She's doing it out of the kindness of her heart.'

'Well it ain't enough, is it? Kindness don't buy food, put money in our pockets. We was better off back at Tanglewood. Why don't she go to her Yankee lover? Joshua says he's here in Savannah, and he's rich.'

Joseph's fingers fastened round her wrist so tightly that she caught her breath in agony. The coal-black features thrust close to hers were grim with anger. The eyes, threatening. She cowered back, suddenly afraid.

'You know nothing about him, girl. Do you hear me? Nothing.' He shook her roughly and pushed her towards the table. 'Get that laid before your man comes back. If I hear one more word from you, I'll have him take a stick to you.'

David Ruell had been at his brother's comfortable house for over three hours. Far longer than he intended when he had arrived, armed with what he considered to be the best of tidings. Jared had been out and had only just returned, so he accepted an invitation to stay and dine.

'Tell me your good news first,' he said, as Jared poured snifters of brandy to accompany the coffee that Pat Wayne had just brought. 'Here I am with the surprise of the year, and you try to pip me at the post! No deal.'

'Why not? The bank manager handling the affairs of Tanglewood plantation was a heavy gambler, you said, by the name of Cauldwell. I recognised the name, but I wasn't too sure it was the same man I knew. Last night I found out that it was. I had a few friends, for want of a better word, here to play a game or two. All pretty heavy betters. Cauldwell was one of them.' Jared relaxed into a chair and lit the inevitable cigar. One of the large downstairs rooms had been converted into a gambling-room soon after he left the army. It provided him with a steady income and, as he was by no means an amateur at cards, often larger windfalls of cash which he considered rightly his as due compensation for the bad luck which had dogged his footsteps since he met Holly Beaufort. 'For me, it was a very profitable evening. Cauldwell ended up owing me a large sum of money.'

'Good heavens,' David ejaculated. 'The man's in debt up to his ears now, and I've just heard on the professional grapevine that he's under investigation by the auditors. Suspicion of embezzling bank funds. Customers have been complaining about their accounts. And then there are these deals with speculators looking for property. It's my guess that he finds suitable places, gets them for back taxes and then sells them at a profit.'

'I know he does. When everyone had gone, I played

a game of bluff. I told him that Richard Mitchell, whom he had helped to get Tanglewood, was a close friend of mine and had suggested I talk to Cauldwell as I was looking for a property round here. Within half an hour he had offered me four places. Most of them in the same condition as Tanglewood. Run down, without labour, available for a reasonable sum. If you checked them, you would probably find they are all up for tax money.'

'Do you want me to?'

'It won't be necessary. Once he had admitted his complicity in Mitchell's acquisition of Tanglewood, I had him where I wanted him. I didn't want his money last night—besides, he'd probably have robbed some poor customer to get it for me—I was after something bigger. I'm not a fool. I wanted—and got—in return for that IOU of his, the outstanding mortgage on Tanglewood. When he realised that Pat had been listening to everything we said, he was also kind enough to sign a letter I had drawn up, admitting that Holly Beaufort had been tricked out of her home. He gave Mitchell the money. They were to split whatever came out of the sale.'

'Congratulations, you old devil!' David swallowed his brandy and held out the glass. 'I'll have another one on the strength of that. Here I am thinking how clever I have been to help you out of a hole, and you didn't need me at all. You always did take care of yourself.' He was serious again, contemplating his brother, knowing that what he had done would not be with his approval. But it was done, and legally. 'You know I never agreed with Father's will disinheriting you. I've done something about it.'

'Like what?' Jared demanded, his eyes narrowing suspiciously.

'We are brothers, and we inherit equally. It's too late for you to change a thing; I signed all the papers yesterday. I'm selling up in New Orleans and making the head office here in Savannah. I'd like to stay here, if it's all right with you?'

'You can have the place. I have no more use for it,' Jared said harshly. 'Go on.'

'Half the money from the sale of the house and land will be yours. Also half of what Father left me—securities, money—I have already deposited in your bank account. The only thing I own totally is the firm. You have no interest in that, anyway.'

'You damn fool, you were a rich man.' Jared glared at him. 'I don't want your charity! I didn't ask for it, did I?'

'Those looks don't frighten me any more, Jared. I'm your brother, remember, and I know you. You've enough money to put this plantation back on its feet, if that's what you want, or to live there in grand style just counting your assets, though that doesn't sound active enough for you. You'll be able to buy yourself a dozen women better than Holly Beaufort. Maybe find yourself a wife . . .'

'Better!' Jared ejaculated bitterly. 'God, man, I wish I could find better.' And suddenly David clearly recognised the demon that had driven his brother since his abrupt departure from the army. 'I've had a dozen women these past seven months, trying to forget her, but her face haunts my dreams, or should I say nightmares.'

'You still love her. That's what this is all about, isn't it?'

'Rot!'

'Truth! She didn't want you, but you love her. There's only one way to deal with that kind of enemy, isn't there, Jared? Total destruction! That's what you want for her. Will it ease the pain? Appease your pride? She must have been some woman. I'd like to have met her.'

'You will.'

'Shall I foreclose on Mitchell? She's in the palm of your hand now. All you have to do is squeeze, and watch her suffer.'

'Damn you, don't make it sound as if I'm going to enjoy it,' Jared retorted. Once he would have done. It was all he had thought about in his prison cell and while he waited for the court verdict. A thousand times he had cursed his love for her, and himself for being unable to eradicate her from his memory. She was with him everywhere he went, every moment of the day and often, as he lay awake, she was in the room with him, haunting him with her unseen presence. Ruthlessly he fought off the moment of sentimentality. His brother was right. She was where he wanted her. Now she would discover what it was like to be manipulated, and helpless to prevent it. 'Invite Mitchell to a meeting here. Offer him what he paid for the place. He'll refuse, of course. That's when you tell him you have the mortgage. Invite her, too.'

'You'll be here?'

'I wouldn't miss it for the world.' Jared's head jerked up towards the door, as they heard a commotion outside and the sound of loud voices. It burst open as he came to his feet. Like a large jungle cat uncoiling himself for the lunge at an enemy, David thought, as he followed suit, and saw his brother's hand reach inside his coat for the pistol he always carried at his waist. It was not drawn. 'What the devil . . .'

The words died on Jared's lips. In the open doorway, one arm twisted behind his back and held in the iron grip of Patrick Wayne, was a tall negro he had thought never to see again. The overseer Holly had placed in charge of the plantation. Run away from his new employer, perhaps, but what was he doing here?

'I didn't know this was your place.' Joshua tried again to free himself from the vice-like grip on his arm, and cried out in pain as Wayne exerted more pressure on it and was still again. 'I didn't know.'

'He came prepared, Major. I think he did.'

The Irishman tossed a pistol into Jared's hands.

'Colt. Army issue. Steal it off a dead Yankee?' he drawled, dropping it on the chair behind him. 'No, Pat, he's got no reason to want to harm me. He may not be top man at Tanglewood nowadays, but he looks to me as if he's working regularly. Fairly new clothes, shoes. Eats well, too.'

'I wish I had known this was your place. I'd have put a bullet in you as you sat there drinking your brandy, Major.' The hate-filled voice broke across Jared like an explosion, and the amusement died in his eyes.

'Did she send you?' he demanded.

'Who? Miz Holly? She don't know you are here. I didn't tell her even after she saw you that day. She thought she was mistaken, and I let her think that. You done enough to her, Yankee.'

'I left her with a house and food to see her through the winter. Even that went beyond my orders.' The memories were returning, and with them, the pain!

'And because of it he was court-martialled and dismissed from the army,' David said coldly, joining in the conversation for the first time. Jared wheeled on him fiercely.

'Stay out of this.'

'Why shouldn't he know what happened to you because you tried to . . .'

'To what? Atone for my sins? Ease my conscience? She didn't understand then, why should she now? Her precious home, that's all that ever mattered to her. She used me.'

'Miz Holly ain't got Tanglewood no more,' Joshua spat the words at him. He cared little for the disgrace Jared had suffered. It was nothing compared to the suffering of the girl he had come to respect, even love in a strange, adoring way. Besides, he had deserved it!

'I know. The fiancé came back and settled for Laurette instead.' The smile on Jared's face was not pleasant, and David looked at Wayne in the hope of understanding the antagonism between these two men, one white, one black. What had happened at that damned plantation? The Irishman caught his eyes, shrugged, and continued to hold his prisoner in an agonising grip.

'He came back all right and Miz Holly took him in when he had nothing. Like you, he used her.' Jared's eyes were suddenly cold grey, chilling in their blankness. Used her! That was funny. 'We was winning. The cotton would have paid the taxes, but it burned, and Miz Laurette, she was responsible for that. I know she was. I saw her talking to them darkies that ran off the same time as it went up in flames, and then Mr Richard came back again. He was master then, paid the taxes himself and him and Miz Laurette got married and told Miz Holly she got to leave . . .'

'Let him go, Pat, I think the pain is addling his brain. Sit down—Joshua, isn't it? Sit down and don't try to be a hero. I've seen too many dead ones these past few years, I don't want another one on my living-room carpet.' Jared stepped away from him, deliberately turning his back on the negro as Wayne released him. From a silver box he selected another cigar to replace the one which had gone out in the ashtray, forgotten when the door burst open, and lit it before seating himself. 'Sit

down, David. Wayne, pour our guest a glass of brandy.
I want him to go on talking, even if it is a fairy story.
Tell me where she is. Now.'

Joshua looked into the hard, sunburnt features,
measured the distance to the door, and knew he would
never reach it alive. Jared's coat was open, the butt of
the Colt nestled at his waist, visible and easily accessible.
The other Colt lay on the chair beside him, out of reach.

It was past ten o'clock and Joshua had not returned.
Holly began to fear that he had been accosted on his
way home, by other negroes or by white vagrants who
haunted the back alleys. The last of their precious
money stolen. The man lying bruised and bleeding,
unable to raise help. Not that anyone would have gone
to his help in these troubled times. Too many people
cared only for themselves, passed by those who bore
scars of suffering or begged in the streets, secure in the
little world they lived in which offered them very little,
but enough to keep the wolf from the door and left
nothing to spare for others, however needy.

With a sigh, she sent Joseph and Mimosa to bed. For
another hour she and Martha sat sewing before the fire,
sometimes talking, but not often. The woman sensed a
strange kind of withdrawal in the silent girl opposite,
and at last withdrew herself, leaving Holly alone with
her thoughts. Thoughts now filled with Jared Ruell. She
tried so hard to keep him out of her mind and her life,
but he intruded into both every single day. Why had
she not had the sense to get Joshua to follow that
horseman and discover whether she had been right or
wrong? Had it been he, she told herself, she would have
gone to him, confronted him with what had happened
to her, for which he was to blame, and then killed him.
The small Derringer with its single bullet was still among

her belongings. Had he not allowed the negroes to go with his men, if he had left more food and grain, or the horses, she told herself she would have survived. But would she? What if another Yankee officer had come along afterwards, taken all the things he had left, and still burned the house? She could not have blamed him for that!

How stupid it was to hold him responsible for the loss of Tanglewood. It had been a casualty of war, just like herself and so many others. Jared Ruell was responsible for only one thing, the unrequited love inside her which refused to die. It rose up to taunt her on nights like this, when she was alone and in a thoughtful mood, to remind her how good it had been to have a man's strong arms about her, to feel the passion in the kisses she had at first refused, then welcomed. To burn in her breast like hungry flames. Flames no water on earth could quench. Only he could do that, and he was lost to her. Wearily, she looked down at the sewing on her lap. Not half finished, but it would be by morning. Perhaps, by then, Joshua would be back. If not, she intended to take Joseph and Mimosa and go to look for him.

Eleven! Where was Joshua? Dead? No, he was strong enough to fight off an attacker, intelligent enough to know if he was being followed through the dark streets. Her heart somersaulted unsteadily as she heard a carriage draw up outside and then the low murmur of men's voices. Something had happened to him. Apprehensively she flew to the door and wrenched it open, gave a glad cry, and stepped back as Joshua bent to duck his head through the low opening.

'Thank heavens, I was beginning to think . . .' Her voice trailed off in disbelief as two more men came after him into the small room. The ground seemed to move so violently beneath her feet that she thought she would lose her balance.

'So you told me the truth. She is here,' Jared said, staring across the table where she had tossed the dress she had been stitching. She was just as lovely as the day she had stood before him in the barn, green eyes flashing with hatred, defiance blazing from the lovely face. Thinner, much thinner, he realised, and then, as his eyes adjusted to the ill-lighted room, he saw how wrong he had been. Lovely, yes. She would always be lovely to him, but she was pale and tired. The long torrent of blonde hair no longer shone, and it was pulled back from the painfully thin face into a tight knot at the base of her neck. Once it had swirled like grains of sand through his fingers, he remembered. Her eyes lacked emotion of any kind, and an ache rose inside him. This was not the Holly Beaufort he had known. This was an uninteresting shadow, trembling as she stared at him. Was this what he had come to wreak his revenge upon?

'What is he doing here?' Her eyes searched Joshua's face. He could not have brought him here. It had to be a mistake.

'I went to this house to sell the ring, Miz Holly. I didn't know it belonged to him. Believe me! He made me tell him where you were . . .'

'Made you! What did he give you? Money?' Holly said bitterly. Betrayed by a friend. 'Judas!'

'No, he gave me nothing. It's what he's going to give you. All of us.' Joshua's face betrayed no expression, even though her words wounded him deeply. He had done the right thing, he told himself over and over again in the carriage. Miz Holly was not meant to sit and sew like a common woman. She was a lady, and Jared Ruell could put her back where she belonged. He had promised. And for himself there would be work, always.

For his father and Mimosa. He had been right. In time, she would see that. When she was back home again, she would thank him for what she now considered a betrayal of her trust.

'I want nothing from Major Ruell! If you have sold yourself and the others to him for his promise of money . . . or whatever it is he has offered you, then don't try to plead your cause by involving me.' Holly was beside herself with rage. It was as if the hunger in her had been so intense it had conjured him out of thin air to mock her with those slate-grey eyes, as so often before. She swayed unsteadily.

'For heaven's sake, you have frightened the poor girl to death,' David declared from the doorway. 'Isn't there any gentleness in you, Jared? Any pity?'

'Pity?' Holly cried. She fought against the shock she had received and, as he stood silent, won her battle. 'Major Jared Ruell gentle? How little you know of him!'

'You are wrong, Miss Beaufort. I am his brother.'

'You have my sympathy, sir.' The pride was back in her voice, and the face she directed towards Jared was full of it also, to remind him of their last disastrous, explosive encounter. For a moment the sight of her had made him wish . . . He dismissed all thought of weakness from his mind. He had come too far to alter course now, and her reception had proved that she harboured not one iota of feeling for him. 'What do you want here, Major? You are not welcome. There is nothing here for you to steal, you know. I know you still have my horse. I'm surprised, she would have fetched you a good price. Your appearance tells me you have fared better than most of us in this house since the war, so perhaps you didn't need to sell her.'

A cold fury swept through Jared at her cruel words. He was unaware of the other woman who came out of a side room, all his attention centred on Holly's accusing features.

'It's plain Jared Ruell. I'm no longer in the army. You and Rhys, between you, put paid to my career. I was stripped of my rank and dishonourably discharged after a court-martial found me guilty of disobeying orders.' He hurled the words at her, and saw her flinch.

'I didn't know. How could I?' she gasped.

'Would you have cared? You wished me dead before I left, do you remember?'

Did she? Those words and the memory of Jared's tortured expression haunted her in a repetitive nightmare.

'You almost had your wish,' he continued, and she realised he had not expected an answer. She, too, had been condemned and found guilty in that long moment of silence. 'The sentence was death. If it hadn't been for a combination of my father's influence and a long-standing friendship with General Grant, I'd have gone before a firing-squad. There was a time when I wished it. Now,' he paused, his eyes on her face, an ugly smile deepening the corners of his mouth, 'now, I'm glad I'm still alive. I should have missed this reunion.'

So that was the reason for seeking her out. For a moment she had hoped. Fool! One look at his face was more than enough to fear his return. Such contempt there for her. He blamed her for the ruination of his career!

'Holly, who are these men? Do you know them?' Martha, silent until now, stepped forward, looking at her in bewilderment. Both spoke like well-bred gentlemen and were well dressed. The diamond ring on Jared's finger caught the lamplight and she caught her breath in envy. Following her gaze, Holly saw it too, and the sight of him wearing her father's ring was like the turning of a knife in her chest.

'I know only one, the other is his brother. I wish to speak to neither. Please make them go, Martha.'

'No, Miz Holly,' Joshua urged. 'Listen to what he has to say before you send him away. He owes you, doesn't he? That's what you believe. Then hear him out. He's offering what you want . . .'

'He has nothing I want. How could you misjudge me in this way?' Holly whispered.

'I know what's in your heart. Where you'd like to be right now. That's the only reason I brought him here.'

'I wish to speak to Miss Beaufort alone. For a few minutes only,' Jared said, and Martha was swayed by the persuasive tone of his voice. If he could help Holly . . . 'I promise you she is in no danger. I am here to help her.'

'Stay,' Holly begged, but the woman nodded and went back to her own room, closing the door firmly. She stood silent, confused, fighting against the urge to sink into a chair. In the lamplight she thought the harrowing experience Jared had been through, which had made him an outcast among society, did not appear to have aged him at all. She could see no grey in the black hair, and the satanic features were as bronzed as she remembered. The broadcloth suit he wore looked new and expensive. His leather boots shone with a dull glow in the muted light, denoting an affluence she found surprising under the circumstances. His eyes were shadowed, guarded, refusing her access to his thoughts as he took the diamond ring from his finger and laid it on the table before her.

'This is yours, I believe.'

'You took everything else from me, why not that?' she flashed, and he stepped towards her with an oath.

'Don't spit fire at me, girl, or I'll turn round and walk out of here,' he snapped, knowing full well that now he had seen her again, he could not.

'Why should you wish to do otherwise? What do you want from me?'

Once he had held her in his arms and they had spoken of love and a possible future after the war. The war was over, but there was nothing for them except memories of betrayal and distrust and deceit.

'So you still have a vestige of Southern pride left,' he mocked.

'And I shall keep it.' Holly's head tilted back proudly, and he saw the dark shadows beneath her eyes. Of fatigue and despair, he realised. She was saddled with three negroes who depended on her. Life was not at all as it had once been for Holly Beaufort, he thought, looking at the work on the table. In offering her an escape, he would achieve his goal. Sentiment and love could go to the devil. He had her where he wanted her, and he would take full advantage of it for fear of losing her again. For whatever reason he could bind her to him . . .

'Do you want Tanglewood back? I can give it to you.'

The words hung in the air between them. He heard her sudden intake of breath, saw the hope which rose in her face, then die as she surmised the price she might have to pay.

'You—you don't have it. Richard Mitchell owns it now.'

'He will sell to me in a very short time. Think of it, Holly Beaufort. Back where you belong.'

'And your terms?' She did not want to hear them—she knew what he would ask. The triumph which gleamed in his eyes confirmed her worst fears. Did she have the courage to pay his price?

'You come with the house.' Behind him, David swore softly. Mimosa and Joseph had come from the back and stood like silent shadows in one corner of the room, rooted to the floor at the ultimatum delivered without mercy. Her lips parted, but no sound came from them. Brutally he pushed home his advantage. 'Think of it. Pretty clothes again. The return of the home you love above everything. When did you last wear silk or velvet? Do you remember?' She did. Both occasions had been while she was with him. That final night when he had held her in his arms and she had asked him to come back to her, but she would not have admitted it. 'Decent food on the table and servants to wait on you. I can put you back where you belong, where I know you want to be—if you are willing to pay my price. Such a small thing in return for my generosity, isn't it?'

Joshua had told him everything, she thought, horrified. Her soul had been laid bare before this man once before, and she had recovered. This time it might not be possible. The things he offered were what she craved. Tanglewood reborn. Her inheritance restored. To live there—with Jared. Mistress of the home she loved. Mistress of a man who despised her, would use her.

'The contempt of decent society and the loss of my pride. How you hate me.' Her voice was hardly audible. Her fingers caught at the skirts of her dress in agitation as she stared at Jared, wishing she had the will to refuse the terrible offer, knowing that she could not for the sake of herself and those who had come to rely on her. For her brothers and her father who had died protecting the way of life they thought they should be allowed to lead in peace.

He wanted her. He wanted revenge for the deceit he thought she had practised on him, the words she had

thrown at him that day. Let it happen. He would be
satisfied once he had extracted his due, and she would
have all she cared for around her. She had to believe
that it would happen, or the sacrifice she was about to
make would be worthless and degrading. One day,
perhaps, he might look at her and realise what was
locked away in her heart. It was a slender hope, but
nevertheless she seized on it.

'Which are more important to you? Tanglewood
and the plantation, or that people will talk about you
behind your back whatever you do?' Jared lit a cigar
and puffed clouds of smoke into the air, one hand
thrust deep into a pocket, as he waited for an answer.
She was going to refuse him! He had not taken that
into account for one moment. Urged on by a force
he did not understand, and refused to accept as pity,
or worse, affection, he added, 'My carriage is outside.
I have offered Joshua his job back as overseer, and
he has accepted. Both Joseph and the girl over there
are welcome to work for me if they wish. I shall need
all the help I can get to get the place back into shape
again. I hear the new owner sits on his backside all
day long, too idle even to supervise the place. He
has an attractive wife, I believe. Joshua had your best
interests in hand when he told me where you were.
He's a good man, even though he does want to use
me as a target. I thought at first it might have been
your idea, but he convinced me otherwise.'

'Me, have you killed?' Holly's gaze was scornful. She
was beaten, not defeated. 'I have not given you a
moment's thought since you left Tanglewood.' She
stared at him, then lifted her shoulders in a gesture
that signalled acceptance. It did not bring Jared the
satisfaction he had been expecting. He wheeled about,
calling for his driver to come and collect her belongings.

'Give me a few minutes to explain to Martha,' she added. 'She has been very good to me.'

'Give her this. She will miss you when you have gone.' Jared thrust several notes out towards her.

Without a word she took them and went into Martha's room. She emerged, tearful, a shawl about her shoulders, clutching a small purse. She looked up into his face, wiped away the last trace of wetness from her cheeks, and squared her shoulders. She brushed past him and went out into the clean night air feeling like a prisoner condemned to a life sentence. Tanglewood was to be her prison. Pray God, she would never come to think of it like that. Jared Ruell, her gaoler. A role he would enjoy. Her steps faltered and she reeled unsteadily on the cobblestones. Joseph hurried forward, but Jared reached her first and put a strong arm about her waist, lifting her up into the carriage.

'It's too late now to have second thoughts, Holly.' His mocking voice came out of the darkness beside her. She felt the hardness of his body easing himself on the seat alongside her. And then, without warning, a merciful oblivion engulfed her, offering an escape from his nearness. The knowledge that he owned her, as she had once owned black slaves. Sold to one Jared Ruell for the price of security.

CHAPTER
NINE

HOLLY REMEMBERED nothing of the drive to Jared's house. She was to discover the next morning that it was in one of the most fashionable avenues in Savannah. A large, imposing mansion built of grey stone with well-kept gardens which reminded her so much of Tanglewood as she walked past the rose-bushes and smelled their sweet perfume.

She had recovered from her faint in a short while, only to find herself in a large bed with Mimosa at her side. She fought so hard to regain control of her composure, but the realisation of what she had done suddenly swamped her!

Jared's appearance at the bedside abruptly curtailed her tears. Although she protested vigorously, and she remembered trying to strike him several times, he forced her to drink a glass of warm milk heavily laced with brandy. So much so that her senses began to slip away the moment he laid her back on the soft pillows. Her brain rapidly became numbed from the alcohol which thankfully absorbed the shock she had received without warning.

'Sleep, Holly. Fight me tomorrow. Not now.' How gentle his voice sounded. He could afford to be lenient now that he had the upper hand. She had given herself into his hands too easily. But it was for Tanglewood! For Joseph and Joshua and Mimosa. Or was it for herself?

Fight him! Yes, she would do that. She must! Even though she had surrendered to his demands, there was still a part of her which would always remain hidden from him. A part he would never own, even though he might possess her body. She loved him still! But how could she? He would never know it, for to reveal this final weakness in the chain of her defences would render her exposed to his scorn and contempt.

'Well now, how did you sleep?' Holly opened her eyes to find Martha standing beside the bed, a breakfast tray in her hands. 'You look better. Sit up and get this food inside you. I have instructions to see you eat every morsel.'

'Martha! What are you doing here?' She pushed back loose hair from her face. The tray deposited on her lap held hot coffee, toast oozing in butter, and eggs on top of slices of ham. There was a small pot of honey beside a plate of extra toast. She had not eaten this well for many months, Holly thought, as she sipped the hot coffee first and felt it stimulating her sleepy brain.

'Mr Ruell came to the house to collect the rest of your things, and then, guess what? He asked if I would like to come and look after you, and then become his housekeeper when he moved on in a few weeks to a plantation he is going to buy. Imagine it!'

'Tanglewood!' Holly bit into a piece of toast smothered with yolk from one of the eggs. The dark recesses of her mind opened up and she saw herself racing away from the house, leaving behind her one of the Yankee cooks covered in egg yolks. She had wanted to laugh then, but not now. There would be other memories which would come crowding back on her the minute she stepped into the house again. Those of her father and brothers, the sight of Lieutenant Rhys filling a sack with ornaments and trinkets. Jared holding her in his arms as they danced on the veranda—and the heat of the flames which had almost destroyed the house. Orders! He cared more for those than he did for her. He had used her, and she must never forget it. It was her only shield to use against the life he planned for her.

'Have—have you accepted?' It would be nice to have her friendly face about her, and she acknowledged the fact that she was going to need all the help she could get in the future.

'How could I turn down such an offer? On the way back, we stopped at Ada's. He had me bring you some new clothes, and didn't even care about the cost. You are expected at her shop this afternoon at four o'clock. He had me make an appointment for you. She's to make you a complete wardrobe. Everything! Do you want to see what I have picked out for you? I did my best.'

Stunned, Holly nodded. So she was to be decked out in the best money could buy. Lace and satin, velvets and brocade. All paid for by Jared Ruell, she thought, as she touched the delicate woven design of the lace and taffeta dress offered for her approval. It was something she must grow accustomed to again. Let him dress her in finery, parade her before everyone in Savannah, for she felt sure that this was the object of the exercise. It would be for a short while only. Soon she could bury herself back at Tanglewood and no one else would matter to her.

'I've eaten enough. I feel lazy lying here. I suppose I must go downstairs.'

If the woman noticed a reluctance to do so, or a disinterest in the clothes shown to her—which would have turned the head of almost any girl of Holly's age in Savannah—she made no comment. Time healed, she thought, gathering them up from the bed. Time was all she needed.

'Where is Mimosa? She should be waiting on me, not you,' Holly protested as the tray was removed.

'Out with Joseph and Joshua. Buying new clothes, too. Why even I have a complete new wardrobe. You should have seen Ada's face when I began picking out dresses for myself! You have yourself a very generous man, Holly. Take my advice and hang on to him. I don't know what happened between you in the past, but I tell you now, his kind are scarce in this world.'

Holly threw back the bedclothes with an indignant exclamation. Generous! Only because it suited him!

'He's a devil! During the war he came to my home and installed himself and his troops there without so much as a by-your-leave and, when they left, he made them burn my crops and barns, and destroy or steal our livestock. We were left with practically nothing!' Her voice often breaking with emotion, Holly told how it had been. Martha listened without interruption until she had finished. 'He's a Yankee. He'll never change! He's out to revenge himself on me because . . . because . . . Oh, it doesn't matter. For some reason he lost his commission and was dishonourably discharged. As if I am to blame for that!' Had it been for another reason, she could have understood, but to blame her for the loss of the life he loved! It was as unforgivable as everything else he had done. 'I don't care what he does to me. Not any more. I shall be living at Tanglewood again, and that's all that matters to me.'

'My brother wore a blue uniform too,' Martha said, as she helped Holly to dress. She took great pains with the long blonde hair, brushing it with a silver-backed brush until it shone. Mimosa had for some time ceased to take such care, Holly realised, and she had been either too tired or too preoccupied to notice her lack of attention. 'I never understood his reasons for going against his family, but it never stopped me from loving him. It's not the uniform, it's the man inside that matters. Remember that, however difficult it is for you. Why did your Yankee major not fire the house? You say it was common practice. Why were you allowed a roof over your head when other poor souls were deprived of theirs? In disobeying a direct order in time of war he was risking his army career and his life, my dear. Men have been shot for less.'

No! Holly thought, mortified. Was that why he had been cashiered? It could not be true. He would not risk everything for a few stolen kisses, the promise to return to her, which meant nothing at all! There had to be another reason which she knew nothing about! Please God, let there be another reason, she prayed, or upon her conscience would be the destruction of a man who had tried to help her. A man she had loved then, still loved, had rejected and yet wished for every moment of her days. His revenge would destroy her as her lack of understanding had him. Was that what he intended? She knew it was, and she had no weapon with which to fight him.

'He looks as if he has come out of this war very well,' Holly said, not wanting to consider the possibility that Jared could have cared for her. 'He promised to come back for me when the war was over, but he didn't, because I meant nothing to him. I—I was a diversion . . .'

It took her another half-hour to gather enough courage to go and face the man waiting somewhere below. She delayed over her toilette, discussed Tanglewood to great lengths with Martha, but did not make a move towards the door until conversation had been exhausted, and both knew it.

The house was impressive. Nowhere near as large as her own, but pleasantly furnished, she saw, and without thought for the cost. Jared Ruell, despite his unseemly and abrupt discharge from the army, still lived in a style she envied. Once she . . .

She went down, and made in the direction of the voices coming from one of the downstairs rooms. From the breakfast-table, where they still sat deep in conversation, Jared and David broke off to stare at her as she appeared in the doorway. She was pale, but in control of herself. She wore one of the dresses Martha had selected for her. The plainest of them all. Jared's mouth deepened into a smile at the sight of the demure silk, buttoned high to the neck. It showed nothing of the delightful figure that had been revealed to him in the watered yellow silk the night before his departure. But it was still the same colour. He wondered if she had realised that?

'Miss Beaufort.' It was David who rose and ushered her to the table, pulling out the empty chair beside his. Jared did not move. 'Would you like coffee? Yes, it is still hot. I hope you are feeling a little better this morning? I gather Jared gave you quite a shock last night.'

'No more than he intended, I am quite sure,' Holly returned. She ignored the devil face opposite, and smiled into that of his younger brother. This one, at least, knew his manners.

'You don't sound very happy, Holly,' Jared remarked quietly. 'I've taken you out of that hole you were living in, provided you with clothes and adequate comfort for your servants. You have, within reason, only to ask for anything else you require. Have I lied to you? I thought I made your position perfectly clear last night. Do you wish to go back on our agreement? If you do, then you are free to leave now and take your dependants with you.'

'Do you have to be so damnably harsh with the girl?' David snapped, pouring Holly's coffee and thrusting the cup into a trembling hand. 'Look at her. Anyone with one grain of sense can see she's near to breaking-point.'

'She is far stronger than you can ever imagine,' Jared retorted dryly. 'Save your sympathy. Well? Do you want to leave?'

'No.'

His eyes gleamed at the swiftness of her answer. 'That suits me fine. I'm content to have you where I want you.'

His insolence momentarily robbed her of speech. Then she said bitterly, 'You don't care for anyone, do you?'

'Jared Ruell. That's who I care about,' came the fierce reply. Ignoring her for a moment, he turned his attention to his brother. 'Isn't it time you were leaving for the office? You may be your own boss, but you have a lot of paperwork to do for me today, remember?'

'I'll be in touch as soon as I have any news. If I don't see you before, I'll be moving in at the end of the week,' David said, rising. He took Holly's hand with an apologetic smile and touched her fingers to his lips. She watched a grim smile crease Jared's features at the gesture, but noticed, too, how cold those eyes remained. He did not like his brother being attentive to her, she thought. He was incapable of jealousy where she was concerned, so he had to be annoyed when someone in the house was prepared to treat her like the lady she was.

When David had gone, they sat and faced each other across the cluttered table. The silence played on Holly's taut nerves. What was there to say to him? If this was how it was going to be when they were together, she would go slowly mad.

'My business here in Savannah will take only a few more weeks, and then we can leave for Tanglewood.' Jared went to select a cigar from the humidor on a near-by table and lit it before returning to his seat. Her eyes followed his movements questioningly. 'I suggest you spend that time replenishing your inadequate wardrobe and acquainting Joshua of your requirements for the plantation. I shall demand little of your time. However, there will be the occasional outing to a theatre or restaurant, when I shall require your company.'

His eyes locked with hers. There was no compassion in them for her. The unfathomable expression made her want to shiver.

'Joshua is still to run Tanglewood for you, then?' she asked in a hollow tone. 'You really meant it?'

'Of course, and you will take charge of the house as you have always done. Anything to do with the plantation itself with naturally be referred to me, as I am paying all the bills. The arrangement suits you?'

She had already committed herself. There was no going back now. She nodded.

'One word of warning, Holly. My quarrel is with you and with no one else. I don't expect honesty from you—we both know you are not capable of that—but, I give you fair warning, never try to cheat me again or I'll break that pretty little neck in two. I have not yet forgotten how I held you in my arms and your body offered more than you were willing to give. I am in a position to take what I want now, whenever it pleases me.'

Silently, cheeks flaming, Holly rose to her feet. She did not need to be reminded of her humiliating position.

He would regret those hateful words to her. Somehow she would pay him back. David, the brother whom she had thought to be rather shy in her company, had been soberly dressed in a dark suit. In contrast, Jared wore a white silk shirt open at the neck, and black riding trousers and boots. Full of confidence, he watched her move towards the door.

'Where is the Holly Beaufort I used to know, spitting fire at Yankee intruders? Have you lost your spirit? Or has your pride deserted you at last?'

'I'm coming back when this war is over and I'm going to make you eat crow . . . I'm going to humble that Southern pride and you'll beg my forgiveness . . . I'll see you on your knees.'

As his words rose in her mind, she bit back a retort. What was the use? She could not hurt him with words, but there were other ways. So he wanted her to have a new wardrobe, did he? Well, he would pay dearly for it. She would spend and spend until he was inundated with bills. For herself, her servants, Tanglewood, Martha.

'I have lost neither, Major.'

'Once it was Jared. People might think we are not the happy couple we pretend if you address me in that way,' he chuckled. 'Madame Ada is expecting you this afternoon. You will look and act the part, even though even minute of the day you are wishing me dead. You will spoil my amusement otherwise. Surely you haven't forgotten how to pretend? You were so good at it once.'

Her hand resting tightly on the door-handle, Holly looked back.

'And just when do you intend to extract your pound of flesh, Shylock?' she asked bitingly.

'The moment we set foot inside Tanglewood again.' Her words did not have the desired effect. 'Enjoy yourself until then. Spend my money as you please, but remember I hold the final accounting and I shall demand my due. You are safe until then. David will be here in a few days, and he is a stickler for propriety. You are safe until Tanglewood,' he repeated.

As the door closed behind her, Jared crossed to the tantalus containing whiskey, poured himself a large one, and tossed it back without appreciation. The second one he drank more slowly, feeling it slide down into his stomach like fire, but without the initial heat of the first flames. If he was not careful, she was going to get to him exactly as she had once before. She had looked so lost, so helpless, so in need of comfort that it had been all he could do to restrain the impulse to take her in his arms and wipe out the past with a foolish, impulsive gesture straight from the heart. It would have gained him nothing. The distrust and suspicion would return to his mind as it did every time he encountered those accusing green eyes. Of what did she accuse him? Because of her, he had been through hell. Lost a career, a home, a father he had always cared for more deeply than he admitted to anyone, even to David. He had lost everything, except his brother. And then, out of the destruction, hell-bent on revenge, he had built a new life for himself, a life that would some day incorporate Holly Beaufort, willing or not. God was on the side of the sinners after all, he thought irreverently as he turned and went upstairs. but his eyes were sad. In them was the sadness of a man whose gain brought him no satisfaction.

'He'll be here at eleven,' David said when he was admitted to Jared's presence in the oak-panelled study. 'He's taken the bait! He'll sell, I know it.'

'You sound the way I should.' Jared gave a humourless smile. 'Your luggage has arrived. You have the third floor. Complete. You could work from here if you like. I'll be gone soon, so there will be no one to disturb you.'

David's expression was almost mischievous as he launched himself into one of the enormous leather chairs which dominated the room and dropped his bulging briefcase on the floor at his side.

'We must not lose touch, Jared. Not ever. I want you—and Holly—here from time to time. Don't desert me. Besides, I shall soon be a man of responsibilities myself. I'm sure my wife will want to meet you—and—and Holly.'

Jared frowned at his awkwardness. Something that had never been between them before.

'You don't like what I am doing, do you?' he challenged.

'As you keep telling me, it's none of my business. I'm just the one making all the vital arrangements so that you can destroy that poor girl upstairs.'

'Poor? She's been under my roof three weeks and, during that time, she's ordered enough clothes to—to clothe an army.' Being a soldier it was the only comparison which came quickly to mind. 'She's ordered a new carriage and a team of horses. Jewellery. The bills are flooding in like tidal waves. Poor! Holly Beaufort can match me any time. At least she thinks she can. I still hold the Ace.'

'Tanglewood.' David grimaced. 'I don't like what she has done to you. Even less do I like what you are doing to her.'

'She is trying to bankrupt me.' Jared gave a slow smile as he contemplated the next few hours. By the end of the evening he would be in possession of what they both wanted. Holly would have Tanglewood, and he would have her. Then would be the time for truth. His face brightened suddenly. 'David—a wife!' he exclaimed.

'I was wondering when you would remember that your poor old brother had good news. I met her back home last year. Selena Hastings. Her father was president of the Hastings Ore Company.'

'I remember. A pompous little man with a moustache that took up all of his face,' Jared chuckled. 'I'm glad for you. Sincerely glad. What more can I say?'

'Promise me you will—be—gentle with Holly, Jared. Otherwise you will destroy what little chance of happiness you have seized now. You will destroy yourself and her. Is that what you seek?'

'Damn you, don't preach at me. I don't know what I want any more. No, that's a lie.' Jared's tone was strained. 'I want her. It's all I have ever wanted.'

David reached for the glass at his elbow and raised it in his brother's direction.

'Then I hope that tonight you will both be satisfied.'

Richard Mitchell blustered and threatened. He had come in answer to a summons from the Savannah lawyer seeking to purchase Tanglewood from him. Or so he thought. After only a few minutes in the luxuriously furnished room to which he had been admitted, he realised that was not the reason at all. A cheque had been laid at his fingertips. Five hundred and forty dollars and a few odd cents. The exact amount he had paid in back taxes for Tanglewood. He had lost his temper and torn it in two, and then Jared had stepped into the room and introduced himself. He had sunk back in his chair, knowing something was terribly wrong. Ruell! He and the lawyer both had the same name. Ruell. Jared Ruell!

The Yankee who had been Holly's lover! It was a conspiracy.

And then, in quiet, unhurried tones, Jared had announced that he knew all about the plan devised to defraud Holly of her rightful inheritance. How the money had come from a dishonest bank manager—who that very morning had committed suicide—to purchase her home and enable Richard to send her packing so that he and his new wife could live in comfort until a gullible fool came along and bought it from him at an exorbitant price.

The man listened, only half believing, a smile creeping into his face at the knowledge that the only man able to incriminate him was dead. Jared allowed him a moment in which to think he was safe before dropping the bombshell about the letter he held, written by the dead Cauldwell, naming Mitchell as his accomplice and confessing freely and without duress to the embezzling of bank funds, adding that he, Jared, now held the mortgage to Tanglewood and was foreclosing immediately unless payment were made in full. Shakily, Richard reached for the documents on the table in front of him, and signed them. He had no other choice.

'One day, Ruell.' He stood by the door, staring with hate-filled eyes at the two men lounging in easy chairs behind him.

'Show him out, Pat,' Jared ordered the man hovering at his elbow. 'Give him a hundred dollars so that he can go back and collect what belongs to him before moving on. Come back afterwards, we have work to do.'

When the Irishman returned, he said, 'I want you to take Joshua and head for the plantation with the wagons of building materials and grain. I don't want that man or his fancy woman on the place when we arrive. Is that clear?'

'Are you asking me to put them off nicely, Major? Or just put them off?'

'When it comes to it, remember how they kicked Holly out. And there's a little matter of some stolen jewellery. Make sure her sister-in-law doesn't take it with her. Have you completed the list Holly gave you?'

'Yesterday. Are we going into the cotton business, Major?' Wayne had spent enough time on a horse during his army years to have learned to appreciate the last few months of not having the hardness of a saddle continually beneath him.

'It's possible. That old riverboat I bought in April may be just what I need to transport supplies and cotton to and from the plantation. The life could have its advantages, you know.'

'For you, perhaps.' The man gave a crooked grin. 'Anything you say, Major. We'll leave first thing in the morning.'

'Good man, that,' David remarked, as the door closed behind him.

'The best. How tough are you? Feel like spending a few hours publicly in the company of the two most-talked-about people in Savannah just now? The food is on me. Michelle's, in an hour. I've already reserved a table.'

'What if he had not signed?' David asked with a slight frown, and his brother looked surprised.

'I really don't know. I hadn't considered a refusal. Had you?'

'Celebrate?' Holly looked puzzledly at Jared as he stood in the doorway of her bedroom. She stayed well out of his way unless he demanded her company for a specific occasion. They ate together, but never stayed long in each other's presence. Always, in the evening, she sat in her room reading or embroidering until dinner. Afterwards she hid herself away again until it was time to retire. Late at night she sometimes heard revelry from below if Jared entertained gambling friends. Sometimes, if she peered through her door, she would see Jared carrying his brother up to bed after an evening spent together drinking and reminiscing.

How she longed for that kind of companionship from anyone, but it was denied her. Joshua seemed quite content to take his orders from Jared, as did Joseph and Martha. Mimosa complained incessantly that she was worked too hard, especially when forced to help out in the kitchen. She thought herself above such menial tasks now. Laying aside her sewing, Holly shrugged her slim shoulders, not wanting to show the slightest interest in Jared's plans. 'What have I to celebrate?'

'The return to Tanglewood. You can leave at the end of the week if you like. Five whole days and then you will be home again. Mistress of all you survey, so long as you do not go against my will, that is.'

The moment of exultation died in her breast. Deliberately spoiled.

'Put on something pretty,' he continued. 'I must have paid for a dress good enough to be seen at the best restaurant in Savannah. Tonight we dine at Michelle's. Good food, excellent wine, and the company of my brother who has helped to make this all possible. Half an hour!'

The same threatening tone as he had used when he had said Patrick Wayne would be sent to fetch her. Now, as then, she dared not refuse. Her closet was full of clothes. She had spent recklessly, hoping to incur his anger, but he paid the bills without a murmur presented to him, and her advantage, small though it was, was lost. Fool to have imagined she could gain one over him, she thought, as Mimosa helped her to dress.

By now she had become accustomed to the stares which followed her whenever she was in Jared's company. His ruined army career was common knowledge, and he was shunned, not always discreetly, by the upper-class circles of society which he often frequented. Despite their attitude, he dined in the best restaurants and attended theatres, in no way allowing their narrowmindedness to influence his way of life. Holly knew that there were many friends of her family in Savannah who stayed clear of her because of his scandalous reputation. Perhaps, too, because of the one she was fast acquiring.

Jared Ruell was good enough to drink and play cards with, to lose money to, but not good enough to associate with Southern womanhood. She could well imagine the whisperings behind fluttering fans and in the coffeehouses. He has seduced the poor girl—or forced her! A good-looking devil with a glib tongue. He knew how to charm the ladies, given the chance. Devil take him! Who would have believed it? Holly Beaufort, daughter of old Colonel John who had died so bravely trying to stave off the Yankee approach to Goldsboro, whose two brothers were buried in unmarked graves somewhere far from home. Living with him and showing no sign of shame! And she the grand-daughter of a titled French aristocrat! Mistress of dirty Yankee trash!

There were no invitations for her to set foot inside the elegant houses along the street, and faces turned away whenever she appeared. How she longed for one friend, and knew that her only friend, now and for always, was home. It would receive her back and welcome her, without criticism, without reproach. Its walls would once again shelter and protect her. How she longed for these things, she thought, as the carriage carried her through the darkness to the restaurant. Beside her, Jared, in evening attire, a white frilled shirt accentuating the swarthiness of his skin, sat smoking. David, opposite, had long since given up trying to draw her into conversation.

Heads turned, whispered comments followed, as she swept through the large room. Every table was full. She saw no one, shut her ears to the sniggers and the openly inviting smiles most of the men directed towards her. She was an open target. Yet, as Jared's hand caught her elbow and guided her towards their table, his touch made her feel less vulnerable. Nevertheless she disengaged herself at the first opportunity. It would not do to let him think she welcomed the slight show of support, if that is what it had been.

He ordered champagne, and then looked around at the sea of faces. With sardonic amusement lighting up his face, he proceeded to acknowledge people at the nearest tables, addressing them by name, enquiring about families, businesses. Many men were not with their wives—or vice versa, Holly suspected from the swift way the conversations were curtailed. Their baleful glares bothered him not at all, and she saw that even David had to hide a smile.

'Was—was Laurette with Richard when you saw him today?' she asked hesitantly, and Jared looked across the table at her to give her his undivided attention.

'Which one are you interested in?'

'Neither! I mean . . .' The insinuation cut her deeply, as he intended.

'They will not be at Tanglewood when we arrive, if that's what's worrying you. Wayne and Joshua will be going on ahead to ensure their departure. I don't want either of them taking it into their heads to do what I never did. You will find the place as you left it, unless they have taken to selling the furniture to live. Your sister-in-law, as I remember, had very expensive tastes.'

'I was thinking of my grandmother's jewels. I would have liked them back, but I don't suppose I shall ever see them again.'

'One piece at least is safe. Or have you forgotten?'

Her eyes were puzzled as she looked at him, and then the colour fled from her cheeks and he saw her fingers clasp together tightly in her lap. So she did remember. He had carried it with him everywhere. It served as a reminder of her lies and treachery—of his own weakness. Reaching into an inside pocket, he tossed a small leather pouch on to the cloth in front of her. With its return, he was giving part of himself that would always be hers.

'Take it. I have no use for it now. I have the real thing.'

Her necklace, Holly realised. Given in love, returned with contempt! With trembling fingers she drew it out, and David gave a low whistle of admiration as diamonds sparkled and emeralds shone with dull fire beneath the light of the chandelier above them. She had never thought to see it again.

Take this when you go, she had said to him. *With it goes my love and the knowledge I shall be here—if you want to return when the war is over.* The deepening twist to Jared's mouth told her that he, too, was thinking of that evening, and she quickly pushed the necklace into her purse.

She wanted to thank him, but was too afraid of a rebuff in front of his brother, who had made it quite plain, when he took up residence in Jared's house, that he did not like or condone the strange state of affairs between them. He had gone out of his way to be nice to her, and she did not want to spoil the evening for him. Later, perhaps, she would find a moment to be alone with Jared, even though that would take all her courage. She could just imagine the sarcasm that would greet when she deliberately sought his company.

'My! My! What a cosy little trio. Celebrating another Yankee success, Major Ruell?'

Richard Mitchell stood swaying beside their table. Holly looked up at him and was shocked at what she saw. His face was blotched and puffy from weeks of continual drinking, which had begun the moment he first began to make plans for the successful sale of the plantation. Anticipation had made him spend heavily, forcing him into credit with merchants in Savannah who were now pressing for payment. Jared, knowing of the circumstances he had allowed himself to sink into, had deliberately made it known that he was about to become the new owner of Tanglewood and would be taking possession personally a few days after the sale. Creditors had been swarming all over Richard since he arrived back at his hotel, with nothing to show for the sale. In desperation he had dived into the nearest bottle, and had then gone seeking what few friends he had left hoping to borrow enough to stave off his creditors until he could slip out of town and return to Laurette. Luckily they still had most of Holly's jewellery. Certainly enough to get them to another part of the country. There was nothing left of the handsome young man who had courted her, she realised. She would have liked to believe it was the war that had turned him into a liar and a schemer, prepared to use any methods to steal Tanglewood from her, but she knew that was not the truth. Even before he courted her, he and Laurette had been lovers and had continued their relationship through the troubled times in Atlanta and Savannah. They had brought it out into the open beneath her own roof. It had all been a deliberate, wicked plot. He wanted the plantation. Laurette wanted him. For a brief while, both had had their wishes. Now it was over, and she must put the past behind her. The future was going to be what she made of it, Holly told herself. A future with Jared, however difficult, was better than one without him.

Richard's brown eyes dwelled at length on the elegantly gowned woman whose hair gleamed like gold, and then, as recognition dawned, they wandered in an insulting fashion down over her bare shoulders to where the dark blue fichu of lace was fastened between the hollow of her breasts with a gold brooch.

'What are you doing here?' he demanded, his voice slurred, and the brandy fumes were so overpowering that she turned her face away.

'She's with me,' Jared said coldly.

Just like that! Delivered without one scrap of regard for her feelings. She knew, as she looked into the eyes of the people near by, that they were all of one mind. Living with a dirty Yankee!

'Resuming the little affair you started at Tanglewood, eh, Major?' His voice was loud enough to carry far beyond their table, and Jared watched her grow rigid with embarrassment. 'Or are you repaying him for the little deal he's just completed, Holly? I should have known something was wrong when you left so suddenly. Came straight to him, did you? You sly little bitch! I wasn't good enough for you, was I? Going to throw me over for a Yankee, weren't you? There's loyalty for you, after all I went through to come back to you.'

'You have a loud mouth and it is annoying the lady,' Jared intervened. 'Go away, Mitchell.'

'You aren't in the army any more, Mr Ruell.

Drummed out, weren't you? I've learned a lot about you these past few hours. Dishonourably discharged for the disobeying of an order during the time of war. We shot men like you in my army, but I hear your daddy was an influential man. Nice to have friends in high places. Was she worth your career?'

'Jared. No!' David's hand fastened over his brother's wrist as Jared looked as though he were about to rise. His eyes were blazing now, his mouth a grim, taut line. 'You have what you want. He can't hurt any of us any more. It's only words.'

Jared looked into the unspoken misery of Holly's eyes and wished with all his heart that he could reach out and comfort her.

'Was it because of Tanglewood?' She almost said 'me', but corrected herself in time.

'Only partly. There were other factors, too. I was sick of the war, you knew that. Rhys tried to back me into a corner over Tanglewood and got more than he bargained for. I was prepared for what came.'

Prepared for death? Holly knew he had been. Her rejection of him had been the final nail in the coffin he had been building for himself for many months, and Rhys had proceeded to bury him.

'I'm sure the consolation you offered more than compensated for his loss,' Richard sneered, swaying over them unsteadily. 'That's more than you ever offered me. I wasn't wined and dined in your upstairs room, and taken to your bed.'

David's hand was thrown off. Jared's fingers curled tightly round the stem of his champagne-glass as he snapped, 'You have five seconds in which to offer an apology for the slur you have cast on the name of my future wife.'

A gasp rose in Holly's throat. Her eyes flew to Jared's

face, but he was not looking at her. His narrowed gaze was on Richard, and there was murder in his eyes.

'Wife! Good God, man, you're not going to try and make an honest woman of the little trollop, are you? Why bother with a ring . . .'

The contents of the champagne-glass splashed across Richard's face, ran down the front of his shirt and soaked the shoulders of his jacket. His laughter was abruptly curtailed. He staggered back, cannoning into a dumb-waiter, and scattered glasses and tableware all round him. Several people hurriedly left their seats as Jared rose to his feet and stepped out into the open. He was filled with an ice-cold, murderous, rage which knew no bounds. Had the man not been drunk and incapable of defending himself, he would have launched into him with his fists then and there. Two waiters rushed forward to haul Richard to his feet again.

'Find yourself some seconds. My brother will act as mine. I'm not prepared to await your convenience as to where and when we will settle this. Sober up and be on the common land behind Parnell's lumber yard at six thirty tomorrow morning. If you aren't there, I'll come after you.' He turned back to the table and extended his hand to Holly. 'I've suddenly lost my appetite; I don't know about you. Let's go home.'

Despite a fur-trimmed cape, Holly shivered all the way home in the carriage while David made repeated attempts, all in vain, to make his brother think again. 'In the morning he won't remember a thing,' he protested. To which Jared replied humourlessly, 'But I shall.' He was determined to fight the duel, she realised, and knew sudden fear. If he was killed, she would be free of him, but she did not want that any more. His wife! He intended to make her his wife! Why had he not mentioned it before, instead of allowing her to believe he intended to keep her at Tanglewood as his mistress only, to be discarded if the mood took him. She could have done nothing about that. But if she wore his ring . . . The relationship was to be a permanent one! Had she not been so concerned over his meeting with Richard in the morning, the news would have elated her.

Perhaps the man would not be sober enough to handle a weapon. Or he would apologise? No, Richard would never apologise to her, not after what Jared had done to him. And if he did not show up, Jared had threatened to find him. The thought chilled her, for she knew it was no idle threat. The moment they entered the house, she sought to detain him.

'Jared.' She laid a gloved hand on his arm and was aware of the suspicion in his eyes as he stared down at her. 'Please don't fight him. He isn't worth it.'

'You flatter yourself if you think I am doing it for you,' came the harsh answer, and she stepped back, her hand falling to her side.

'I know better.' She fought back a rush of tears and her voice was unsteady. 'I wish I could be in his place tomorrow, do you know that? At least a bullet through the heart would kill me quickly.'

Picking up her skirts, she went upstairs without a backward glance, unaware of the stricken look in Jared's eyes as they followed her until she had disappeared from sight.

'You could have stopped this thing between you,' David said, wondering if he would ever again see such naked pain in his brother's face. 'She gave you a chance. Why didn't you, for heaven's sake?'

'I didn't know how,' Jared said. As David took a step towards him, understanding registering in his expression, he turned and went into his study and shut the door.

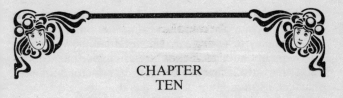

CHAPTER
TEN

SHE DID not care what happened to him, Holly thought
savagely, thrusting her feet into her slippers and reaching for a robe. She would not show the slightest concern
if he arrived back wounded and bleeding. Not care?
Why then was she up at the crack of dawn, listening for
the return of the carriage? She had tried to stay awake,
but had fallen asleep just before three o'clock, stretched
out across the bed, still fully clothed.

Quietly, so as not to disturb Martha, whose small
room adjoined her own, she stole downstairs and into
the sitting-room. It was scarcely light outside. A heavy
dew still clung to the purple bougainvillaea creeping
past the window and the sky was heavy with rain-clouds.
Dark grey like his eyes! Quickly she turned away, direct-
ing her thoughts elsewhere. Joshua and Patrick Wayne
were leaving for Tanglewood today, and in a few days
she would follow. Home again. She said the words softly
to herself, lovingly. Home again where she belonged.
Mistress of Tanglewood once more, but also Mrs Jared
Ruell. Unless . . .

A carriage stopping outside! Voices. Sudden light
blazed into the room and she rose quickly from the
couch and hurried out into the hall. David was support-
ing his brother, whose left arm hung limply by his side.
With growing apprehension she saw that the whole side
of Jared's jacket was soaked with bright red blood.

'Thank God, you are alive,' she breathed, and both

men stopped their slow progress towards the stairs and looked at her.

'No thanks to you,' Wayne growled as he slammed the door shut after them. 'Almost got himself killed, he did. Get yourself upstairs, Major. The doctor's following close behind. He'll be here any minute.'

'The prodigal returns,' Jared said with a crooked smile which ended in a painful wince. Then his eyes grew puzzled as she moved into the light and he saw that she wore a shift, not a nightgown, beneath her robe, betraying the fact that she had not been to bed. 'If you are going to shed tears over the departed soul of your ex-fiancé, I'd rather you did so out of my sight,' he added, as a single teardrop rolled unnoticed by Holly down over her cheek.

'You fool! You blind fool! I never loved him as I love you.'

Her words thudded into Jared's already weakened body with the force of a cannon-shell. Despite the ministering of a very able doctor after Richard's bullet had torn through his side, he had been bleeding all the way home and was feeling extremely light-headed. Love, she said. It was not possible!

What had she said when he had asked her to trust him that day? Tried to convince her that everything he had told her the night before had been no lie. *'Oh, that! You did not think I was serious, did you? Two can play at that game.'* And she had laughed as she tossed the insult at him. What game was she playing now? Dammit, he was so weak he could hardly stand. Wayne hurried forward to help to support him, brushing Holly aside as she, too, started in his direction.

'You are being very foolish, Holly,' Jared said in a harsh whisper. 'I warned you what I would do if you ever tried your tricks with me again.'

'It's the truth.' Holly stood her ground, wishing she had had the courage to face him like this before. She would not allow him to destroy her love, or to degrade it. She would fight to retain the purity of it, the sweetness it had once contained for a short time, as valiantly as she had fought for Tanglewood, which, until he had entered her life, had always been predominant in it. 'I did not lie to you before. I am not lying now. I still love you.'

'You are reconciled to it, then?' Jared ignored David's urgent grip on his arm. Of course, he was going to make her a respectable married woman. Safe!

'To what? Our farce of a marriage? I suppose I must be grateful I shall have the benefit of a ring. Had you need to salve your conscience, Jared? Were doubts beginning to creep into your mind that you were as wrong about me as I have been about you? I was willing to give myself to you once before, if you remember, and there was no talk of marriage between us then.'

Holly did not flinch beneath the withering gaze directed at her. She had told him the truth. If he refused to accept it, there was nothing she could do.

'I think you had better let them take you upstairs, Jared.' Her voice softened. All the anger and bitterness had drained from her with the confession. Wayne was looking at her in sheer disbelief. There was a faint smile on David's face, and she knew he believed her. One friend, at least, she thought thankfully. Jared's thoughts were locked away behind a mask of pain which threatened to render him unconscious. This was the second time she had, deliberately and foolishly, dropped her defences. She had pretended concern for him when they came home earlier. Pretended? God, what was he to think? His mind reeled as dark recesses opened up, flooding it with memories. 'You blind fool! I love you.'

He loved her! He wanted her desperately, as ardently, as he had that first moment when he saw her standing on the porch with Joshua and Joseph guarding her. Like some golden pagan goddess guarding the entrance to her world. He had stepped over the threshold into that world and known love, but also lies and deceit, mistrust, and a desire for revenge that had almost destroyed them both. Could still do so . . . Holly cried out in alarm as he sagged in the grasp of the two men holding him, but he did not hear her.

David came into the sitting-room an hour later and found her standing by the window. It was light now, a dull, rainy day which did nothing to lift the heaviness pressing on her heart. The doctor had come and gone, but she had been turned away from the door of Jared's room by a sour-faced Wayne, who told her rudely that her assistance was not required. Turned away like a servant. Had she not been so shocked by Jared's collapse and the blood that had stained the stairs as he was carried away from her, she would have reminded the man of his place, that she, as Jared's future wife, gave the orders, not he. Wife! Perhaps that would never happen now.

'Drink this.' David held a glass of brandy beneath her nose and she took it without protest. 'Drink it,' he repeated, and she did so mechanically, dreading the worst. 'He's weak from loss of blood, as you can imagine, but the doctor thinks he'll be well enough to get up in a few days. Wayne says he's seen bigger holes than that in Jared, and he'll be up within two days.'

'He didn't believe me,' Holly whispered. 'I was a fool to have said anything.'

'Someone had to, before this went too far. Finish the brandy and then relax. We have to talk.' David helped himself to a drink and then led her to a chair. 'Jared doesn't know how to stop what he has started. You realise that, don't you? He had it all clear-cut in the beginning. You and Tanglewood and he. It sounded simple, but life is never simple. Fate has had some unpleasant shocks in hiding for you both. Hasn't there been enough hate for you both, Holly?'

'I wished him dead. The day he left me, I wished him dead,' she whispered. 'I killed his love. He did love me, then, I realised that tonight, but I thought . . .

'He hasn't stopped loving you. That's what drove him all these months, but there's a great deal of anger and bitterness intermingled with his love. Just now I'm not sure which will prove the stronger. Which Jared will emerge from tonight. The one who went off to war, the brother I loved, or the one who came back, disillusioned, empty, his career gone, his life in ruins, without meaning.' David leaned towards her, gently took her hands in his. 'Make him believe in you again. It's his only salvation and perhaps yours, too.'

'It's too late. I saw his eyes when I said I loved him. Oh, David, he was remembering the day he left Tanglewood, I know it. He asked me to trust him, and I sent him away wishing him dead! He will never forgive me for that. I can never forgive myself. While I waited for him now, I kept thinking that perhaps God meant to take him from me as punishment for what I had done.'

'Your punishment, if you want to call it that, is going to be living the rest of your life with him,' David chuckled, and saw sudden hope rise in her expression. 'It isn't going to be easy, any of it. You must start now, never regret an instant of what has gone before or will come in the future. Your future. Yours and his and that of your children. Build on the ruins, Holly.'

Build on the ruins as hundreds, thousands, of Southerners just like herself were doing. Build stronger, to last longer. Never to be toppled again. Her future and Jared's. How good that sounded. Impulsively she kissed him on one cheek, and laughed as a slow flush crept into his face. He was pleased at the sound, because it told him she had won her battle. He prayed that, upstairs, Jared had both the strength and the good sense to win his.

'You are right, it isn't going to be easy. I have to show him how much I love him and not just . . . Well, you know what I mean. To share his bed is not enough. He must know that my love makes me proud to be seen with him wherever we are.'

'You have a positively mischievous look in your eyes. What are you contemplating?' David murmured. 'Can I help?'

'Will you take me out tomorrow? There are a few additions I must make to my wardrobe before I go home. I'm going to have a wedding gown made that will keep the female population of Savannah gossiping for a whole year, and I'm going to invite most of them to see me wear it when I marry Jared. All my so-called friends who have turned their backs on me while I was here. I wonder how many will come when I am at Tanglewood again.'

'They will come, if only out of curiosity,' David warned her, but she lightly shrugged her shoulders.

'That doesn't matter. I will draw up the list in the morning and have invitations printed. One set for my engagement ball—every Southern girl has the most wonderful ball to introduce her man,' she explained, as his face registered incredulity, 'and another set for the wedding. I don't care what their reasons are for accepting, so long as they come and see how happy I am to stand beside Jared and become his wife. I want him to look at me and believe, David.'

'If he doesn't, he's exactly what you said he is. A blind fool.'

'I shall still love him even then,' she whispered. 'No matter what!'

'He always told me the best defence is attack.'

'I am about to attack with everything at my disposal. If I lose this battle . . .'

'Why not try and talk to him again,' David urged. 'I'll even come and referee for you. You've got him just where you want him at the moment.'

'That's exactly why I intend to say nothing to him.'

'A sneaky surprise attack once you are within your own territory again,' he chided. 'I think Jared could very well be forced to retreat.'

'He might find the terms of surrender most pleasing. Thank you, David. You have been very kind to me since I came here. I consider you one of my few real friends.'

'I've come to feel the same way about you. I know you could make him happy if he gave you the chance,' came the sincere reply. 'Go in and win, Holly. I'll be backing you all along the line. By the way, Jared didn't kill him, you know.'

'Who?'

'Mitchell. He turned up late, still partly drunk. I think he had started drinking again as soon as we left him last night. Jared refused to fight him. Turned his back and walked away. Said he wasn't worth a bullet. Mitchell shot him from behind. I killed him, Holly. When Jared fell, I thought he was dead. I grabbed up his pistol and fired in a blind rage. I've never felt such anger as I did then. No one could have stopped me.'

* * *

Holly opened the door of Jared's room and peered inside. From a chair beside the bed, Patrick Wayne turned to look at her, his face registering instant displeasure.

He had resented her presence in the house from the moment she had arrived, she realised. Jared had told her, with warmth in his voice, how the sergeant had deliberately picked a fight with Lieutenant Tim Rhys after the court-martial verdict was announced and, within months, was knocking on the door in Greenbank Avenue, seeking employment with his now ex-commanding officer. He had lost his stripes for the last time.

'He's asleep,' he said ungraciously. 'You can do no good here, Miss Beaufort.'

Bristling at the unwarranted insult, Holly entered the room, ignoring him, and stepped to Jared's bedside. He lay so still that for a moment she was alarmed, until she saw his quiet and even breathing. A stray lock of black hair had fallen across his forehead. She bent and brushed it gently away, then drew quickly back lest she had disturbed him, but he did not move. His skin had an unhealthy grey tinge to it and there were beads of perspiration on his forehead. It was the first time she had ever seen him rendered so incapable of defending himself, so helpless. At her mercy, if she wished it. Confined to his sick-bed, he would have to listen to her, but she knew that was not the way to go about it. He would only despise her further for taking advantage of his condition. She had to prove to him beyond the shadow of a doubt that she was sincere, her love steadfast and true.

She saw the first streaks of silver just beginning to show themselves at his temples. They had not been there when he was at Tanglewood. Drawing up a chair, she sat down close enough to reach out and touch him, although she did not attempt to do so again.

'I am staying for a while.' It was framed as a statement of fact, not a request to the silent man opposite.

'Suit yourself. The doctor gave him something to make him sleep, so he won't know you're here,' Wayne answered brusquely, his tone indicating his resentment of her presence.

As the morning wore on, sunlight crept in through a side window, sending little rivers of gold across the bed. The rain had stopped, Holly thought, as she stretched cramped limbs. Had she been dozing? She had no idea of the time. Incoherent mutterings were coming from Jared's lips. Wayne waved her back to her seat as she came to her feet anxiously.

'He's been like it for the past hour. There's nothing you can do.'

Strange names, strange-sounding places, over and over again. Jared's pillow was soaked with sweat, and it ran in tiny rivulets down his face and neck. She wrung out a cloth in cold water and laid it across his burning forehead.

'Do you understand him?'

'Oh, yes, we were there together,' Wayne answered.

'Where?' she asked in exasperation. If Jared's temperature increased, she was going to send for the doctor. 'Tell me, please. I must know.'

'New Mexico in 1859, or was it 1860? Never did have a good head for dates. Not that they matter.' The man sat down again and began to talk. Holly thought he needed to talk about Jared and the past as much as she desperately wanted to hear about this side of the man she loved. With Jared's laboured breathing between them, he told her of the raw captain that had arrived fresh from West Point. How he had quickly earned the respect and admiration of the men under him for the way he fought alongside them, instead of giving orders from the rear. Knowledge of what Jared had been like in those days would give her an insight into so many things she had found puzzling, sometimes almost frightening, in his manner. Wayne, as he spoke, stared down at the man in bed with utter devotion on his face. There was no denying that Jared was the most important thing in his life, too.

He told her of the trouble with the Navaho Indians and the Mexicans, of Jared's friendship with the chief, Manolito, which earned him a sharp rebuke from his superiors, especially when he began to speak on their behalf over grazing rights of which they had been deprived by the erection of a new fort in the area—Fort Defiance. Jared had gone to Washington and enlisted the help of his father's powerful friends, but in vain. In attempting a reconciliation between army and Indians, he had been captured and tortured, and escaped with his life only thanks to the intervention of Patrick Wayne, who went alone into the enemy camp to rescue his commanding officer. He spoke of Jared's growing disgust at the army's treatment of Indian women and children, the callous killing of young men without cause. How, even after his narrow escape, he attempted again to secure peace and, because of his efforts, again all in vain, was transferred back to a desk job where he could cause no more embarrassment. He had left the army then, and resigned his commission, but after only a few months Fort Sumter was fired upon and he was back in uniform. All to please an ageing father who had fought in the defence of New Orleans as a boy of fourteen and had then served with distinction years later in the Mexican war. Jared had been too proud

of the family tradition, of his father, to walk away
from another war he knew would also disgust him.

So that was the story behind Jared's refusal to destroy
Tanglewood. He had seen too much blood, death and
killing years before. He had tried to help then, and had
failed. He *had* helped her, but she had misunderstood
in her distraction and horror and had blamed him for
something not of his making. *He* did not give the orders,
he only carried them out, but she had accused him of
enjoying what he did, taking advantage of lonely
women, stealing to furnish his own pocket. How those
words must have seared him! The final insults she had
hurled into his face as she pretended she had been
playing a game with him had hardened his heart to such
a degree that no remedy on earth could possibly melt it
again. At least she understood. If she did not succeed
in her daring venture, at least she knew now why he
had become so callous and embittered.

For three days Jared remained in bed, the last one
complaining incessantly that he was well enough to get
up. Only Wayne's insistence kept him where he was.
Holly spent the time well. With David's help, she arranged for the printing of invitation cards. One set
for the engagement ball, the most lavish she had ever
organised, another set for her wedding. She had decided
to be married on the first day of January; a perfect
beginning to the New Year. She would need all the time
she could get to arrange accommodation, transport,
the banquet after the wedding ceremony. Tanglewood
would come alive with the celebrations and her happiness. No expense was to be spared! She inwardly winced
at the bills accumulating for payment, her wedding
gown, trousseau, servants for the house, new furnishings
and goodness knows what else, but she stacked them

all into a neat pile and decided that Jared would be presented with them at Tanglewood, not before. She wanted nothing given away until the last moment.

· But when she came back from a fitting towards the end of the week, she found the door of her bedroom open. Closets and drawers were flung wide open and it was very obvious the contents had been closely inspected. Martha came rushing in, close on her heels.

'I tried to stop him, Holly, but he barged in here like a wild bull, wanting to know where you were. When I said you were at another fitting . . . Well, you can see. He went through everything, counting the cost, I think, and then he found a sheaf of papers on the table.'

'Oh, no! I meant to take them with me,' Holly said, her hand flying to her mouth. 'Whatever must he think?'

'That you are going to make the most of your position as his wife, now you have Tanglewood back again,' David declared from the doorway.

'Where is he? I must explain. He mustn't think the worst of me, not now.'

'He's gone and taken everyone except Martha and me with him.'

'Gone?'

'Tanglewood. I'm to bring you when you have exhausted your spending spree. His words, not mine.'

'But he's not well enough to travel. Oh, the fool! He'll spoil everything,' Holly declared, sinking into a chair.

'He expects you to follow in a day or two.'

'Does he now! I won't travel for at least another week,' Holly said, her lips tightening determinedly. 'I've come too far to stop now.'

'Don't talk that way. You sound like Jared,' David said with a frown. 'He's expecting you.'

'Mr Wayne will take care of him until I arrive.'

'You crafty little minx, you and old Pat have cooked something up between you!'

'No. We have simply acknowledged that Jared is the most important thing in both our lives. You can book passages for us in six days,' Holly said. 'I should be ready by then.' And by that time she should have received some answers to the first invitations. Thank heavens that the stationery bills had not showed precise items, or Jared would have known what he was in for.

Her ball-gown would be ready in two days. Possibly her wedding dress and veil the day after. Madame Ada had spared no time and effort in keeping to Holly's schedule. It had cost her dear, or rather Jared, but it would be worth it to see his face. *Oh, Jared, how I love you,* she thought, as she lay in bed that night, and her thoughts were of him at Tanglewood. *Love it as I do. Love me as I love you.* She fell into a blissful sleep, her lips curved into a smile as she watched herself approach Jared on their wedding day, in white taffeta and lace.

It had not changed. Nothing. The lawns were badly in need of attention, weeds grew at the sides of the drive, but the house itself, looming up before her, seemed to welcome her in the brilliant fire of the dying sunset which spread a crimson glow over its white walls. Everywhere she could see that work had been in progress since Jared's arrival. Men and women were bent in the adjoining fields, the stables looked as if they had been totally repaired, and a great joy swept through her as she saw her very own mare being led back inside by a small negro boy. He had returned the horses he took! She had thought them sold long ago. *Jared, how I have misjudged you! As you have me. Please, please let it end in this place I love so dearly. We have so much to offer not only each other, but this land, which is my heritage, which you have returned to me.* It no longer mattered to her that he owned it. She was to share it with him, it was sufficient!

Painting had begun on all the outbuildings and on part of the house itself. Several negroes were planting little border plants in the flower-beds outside the windows of the veranda in readiness for an early spring. She suddenly went so pale that Martha leaned over and slipped an arm round her shoulders.

'What is it, my dear? You look so strange.'

Holly encountered David's gaze on her. He knew the bitter-sweetness of this homecoming. Apart from Jared, perhaps he was the only one who knew what it really meant to her.

Two riders came out of the bank of trees to her left. Joshua and Jared, chatting together like old friends. One was now the overseer of her home, the other its master. By the time the carriage rolled to a halt in front of the house, they had dismounted and were standing on the steps to greet her. Joshua slightly behind Jared, who stood with feet apart, hands thrust deep into the pockets of his riding breeches, reminding her, in a moment of nostalgia, how her father had once looked when awaiting the return of her mother from a visit.

He was still pale, she saw, as David helped her to alight, but the air from the river had considerably darkened his skin, so that only she, who was looking for it, noticed the pallor. The grey eyes fastened on her betrayed no expression. He was going to make it as difficult for her as he could, she realised, and she could do nothing about it for another two days.

'David! It's good to see you.' A smile and a warm handshake for his brother. For her, a mere inclination of his head. 'You have arrived at last, Holly.'

'You sound as if you begrudge me a few more days in Savannah,' she returned with a smile that hid the ache in her heart at his cool reception. 'A girl's wedding day is the most important day of her life, Jared. Would you deprive me of mine?'

'Not at all, so long as you remember there is to be an accounting between us.'

She saw David's eyes narrow angrily as he laid a hand on his arm, and she smiled into the hostile face before her.

'Rest assured, you will be paid in full. We Beauforts have never welched on a deal in our whole history. I hope you will be satisfied with what you receive.'

Tit for tat, until the time came for her to reveal her carefully-laid plans.

'What I have received are acceptances to invitations I never sent out,' came the stony reply. 'To the engagement ball of Miss Holly Beaufort to Mr Jared Ruell. Devil take it! Who are all these people?'

'Friends.' Holly could have broken down and wept in front of him. The acceptances were coming in, she cared not why. Let them gawk at her, let them whisper and gossip behind fluttering fans—this was what she had hoped for, and it was coming true. 'Am I not allowed an engagement ball, Jared? In the South it is the custom, you know.'

'And the wedding invitations?'

'You did say we were to be married, or was that a momentary weakness on your part? I am quite willing to become your wife. I have told you that.'

'Now that you have Tanglewood back,' Jared retorted heavily, but she did not rise to the bait. Let him wait and wonder. Time was on her side.

'No, Jared. *You* have Tanglewood. *I* am merely something you acquired along with it. Wasn't that how you planned it? I am very tired. I shall go upstairs and rest before dinner.'

'I suggest you take the time to tell your servants what to do with the abundance of tents and awnings that have been arriving for the past few days.' Jared's voice followed her inside. 'You arranged all this, then you can damn well organise everything. I'm damned if I'm going to take part in your party games. I'm not here on display.'

Oh, but you are, my love, Holly mused as she slowly went upstairs. *We both are, and you will understand in a little while.*

'Miz Holly!' Joseph came running up behind her, breathing heavily as she stopped and faced him. He was no longer young, Holly thought, looking into the lined face, yet he was as much a part of Tanglewood, as much a part of her, as her dead family, David and Jared. 'Welcome home!'

For the first time in all her twenty years, Holly bent and laid her lips against his cheek.

'We are all home, Joseph. Come and tell me all your news.'

'The master is fuming at the things you ordered. I told him you knew about them, but he's still smarting, Miz Holly. Miz Laurette he sent packing, but he made her leave your jewellery behind. Gave her a railroad ticket back to Atlanta.'

The master! Yes, he was that, and she was proud of the fact. She thought of the organising, for within a day people would begin arriving for the festivities. It was no mistake on her part that she had left her arrival until now. She wanted to give Jared no time to cancel the arrangements she had made. She was backing him into a corner, she realised, as she sat in her sitting-room that evening with Joseph and Joshua, and Mimosa, who seemed to have grown up within the short space of time they had been apart. She carried Joshua's child. The prospect of motherhood. One day she would be so, Holly thought. One day, her children and Jared's would play on the lawn, and Joseph or his son would teach them to ride. They would grow up in a world that had changed and yet was, outwardly, the same. Tanglewood would be their inheritance, as it was hers. She hoped they would be as proud of it as she was, and fight for it as she had done, and go to bed at night listening to the wind in the trees outside, comforted, secure, at peace. This was the peace she had dreamed of for many months. Jared had given it to her without meaning to. Nothing was too great to give to him in return for such a magnanimous gift.

The servants she had engaged before leaving Savannah had been well trained by Joseph before her arrival, and Joshua had done the same with the field hands. The following day marquees were erected on the lawn, accommodation for over a hundred people. She had sent out exactly that number of invitations and had received fewer than half back as acceptances. Undaunted, she ordered cook to prepare the already planned menus for the next three days. Mostly a cold fare, which could be eaten with relish, or held over until the next day. Jared was noticeably absent when the first carriages rolled up to the house, but he deigned to appear at supper that evening, and she could find no fault with his manners. He was charming to her friends, the senators newly appointed in Savannah, and their gauche wives, merchants whose business had supplied much of the merchandise for the restoration of Tanglewood, distant relatives who overlooked Holly's scandalous behaviour enough to

come and stare at her future husband. It was grim
for them both until the actual day of the ball, but
somehow they both came through it unscathed.

Holly's magnificent dress was spread across the bed.
It was a creation of frothy silver and white lace, cut
daringly low. She had chosen to wear the diamonds he
had bought her. Her entrance would stun him, she
thought in satisfaction.

'Pretty,' David remarked, and she looked at him in
alarm. He had come to wish her good luck.

'You don't think it good enough?'

'It isn't the way he always sees you. Yellow silk, with
emeralds at your throat, your hair cascading down your
back like golden sunbeams.'

She caught her breath. He had not forgotten that
night. It had meant something to him. Aghast, she
looked into David's brown eyes.

'Don't tell me this if it isn't true? You don't know
what that night meant to me.'

'I know what it meant to him! Here, he told me to
give you these. Perhaps they will convince you. You
have won your battle without firing a shot, Holly.'

She opened the envelope he handed her and found
herself staring at the deeds to Tanglewood—in her
name. Wordlessly, she looked up.

'I drew them up that way. He never wanted this place
for himself, only for you. If you are not careful, you
will lose him. If you don't make him believe in your
love tonight, there will be no wedding. He'll be out of
your life. You said you love him, but he can't accept it.
Don't you understand that? He wants proof.'

'But I'm giving him that,' she protested, not understanding. 'These people are my proof.'

'He sees you as mistress in your own home, with your
friends about you, or people who may be of use to you

in the future. He thinks he has given you all you want, Holly. That there is no room in your life for him!'

'Oh, David! I thought I was beginning to know him.'

'A few weeks! My dear girl, he is a most complex character. Try spending the rest of your life with him. Even then, you may not succeed. What shall I tell him?' David asked, his hand on the door knob.

'I shall be down very soon.'

'My congratulations, Jared. A magnificent occasion,' David remarked, helping himself to another glass of champagne from a passing servant. 'The life will suit you.'

'I doubt it. My boat is anchored at Jackson's landing. I was thinking of cruising the coast for a while. It would turn into quite a profitable enterprise, you know—restaurant, gambling-tables . . .'

'You're a fool if you leave,' his brother remarked quietly.

'I'm a damned fool if I don't. This grand affair has shown me that. She had to turn the knife one last time, didn't she?' Jared said, tight-lipped.

'Did she?' David's attention was suddenly focused on the top of the stairs, and at the smile on his face, Jared turned to look also and froze, unbelieving.

She was wearing the same dress, yellow watered silk, and at her throat was the emerald and diamond necklace he had returned to her at Michelle's. Her hair was a cloud of sunlight about her shoulders as she descended slowly, as though waiting to catch one particular eye. She had his full attention. To see her that way brought back the memory of that night. The softness of her against him, her eager lips beneath his. The offer of her body! She was doing the same thing now, in full view of everyone. Coming straight towards him, with no interest in anyone else. He doubted if she even saw the guests she had taken great pains—and expense—to invite. Such pride blazing out of her lovely face.

'Oh, my God!' Jared ejaculated, and David looked at him with a nod.

'At last you understand. Go to her, man. Don't let her do it all alone.'

He needed no further prompting. Without being aware of it, he was by her side, her hands were in his and her face was upturned to his, the green eyes shining with love.

'Jared, don't go. If you do, I shall follow you.'

'And leave Tanglewood?' he mocked softly, without meaning to hurt her.

She smiled through a mist of tears, which made the greenness of her eyes like a bottomless pool of cool, inviting bliss.

'Don't,' she pleaded, and immediately he was contrite.

'You have chosen the damnedest time to do this, you little witch! Everyone is looking at us. We have to mingle.'

'Later,' Holly murmured, her fingers closing possessively over his arm. 'I want you to do something very special for me. Something I would not dream of asking another living soul.'

'Anything.' He meant it. At that moment he would have granted her the earth, had it been available, to lay at her feet. That dress, the necklace, the memory. Such a precious memory, and it had been the same for them both. 'Like a real Southern gentleman.'

She ignored the laughter in his voice. 'Will you take me somewhere and show me how much you love me?'

'How very indiscreet—and unladylike, Miss Beaufort, but I shall, with great pleasure. But not now.

Later, when we have appeased all these anxious, if not outraged, faces about us. Do you realise you have not acknowledged a single soul?'

'I have acknowledged you,' Holly whispered. 'No one else matters. They were for you, to prove to you how proud I would be in your company. I wanted everyone to see us together.'

'Oh, God!' Jared groaned and drew her into his arms. Somewhere in the background the musicians had the good sense to strike up a tune, and he guided her onto the floor as though they intended to dance. Couples followed them, and she heard him chuckle. 'Look at them! Like hungry wolves waiting for the kill. Oh, Holly, what an engagement ball you have given yourself!'

He bent and kissed her in the middle of the floor, and fans fluttered and faces grew red, but Holly did not even notice. David helped himself to more champagne and drank their health in a solitary silence.

'Jared, don't. Everyone is looking at us.' Her protest was half-hearted.

'Let them. We shall tell them to go to hell if they don't like what they see. At least we are open and honest! I am what I am and I'm proud of it,' he challenged, and her head came up to acknowledge the same pride swelling inside her.

'I love a Yankee and I'm proud of that, too, and not ashamed. I shall build on that foundation. And you, Jared?'

The question was asked hesitantly, and his arms tightened around her until she could scarcely breathe. They came to a halt, not heeding the amazed faces, the music, the elated chatter.

'If you don't know now . . .'

'Some of them will never understand, you realise

that, don't you?' she said a trifle sadly. 'You will always wear a blue uniform and I shall have betrayed my Southern blood. It doesn't matter, so long as I have you.'

'And I have you, here in my arms where you have always belonged,' Jared whispered tenderly. 'They will never see or understand the chains that bind us. Chains of love. Most of them have never been fortunate enough to have known love.'

His mouth on hers sent the room reeling about her. She thought of the wedding gown locked away in the closet upstairs, and the banquet she had planned as their wedding breakfast.

'Oh, Jared, all those bills,' she said weakly, her fingers entwined in his dark hair. The music had long since stopped. People just stood and stared, but she was unaware of them or their interest. Jared was her whole world.

'The final accounting, remember? The South did not lose after all, did it, my love? You have achieved a major victory, and I willingly concede defeat.'

Another bouquet for the Rose of Romance.

A Highly Respectable Marriage by Sheila Walsh has won the 1984 Romantic Novel of the Year award. Which only goes to prove, once again, that Mills and Boon are the leaders in romantic fiction.

Award yourself a bouquet soon – A Highly Respectable Marriage is available from 11th January 1985, price £1.50.

The Rose of Romance.

Romantic Novel of the Year